Knights, Beasts and W

DISCARDED

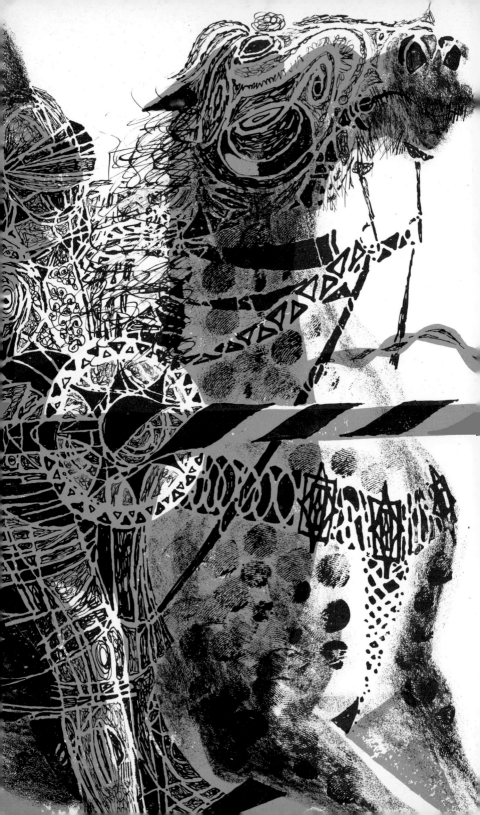

Margaret J. Miller

KNIGHTS, BEASTS AND WONDERS

Tales and Legends from Mediaeval Britain

Illustrated by Charles Keeping

DAVID WHITE · New York

Also by MARGARET J. MILLER,
published by Brockhampton Press

THE QUEEN'S MUSIC
THE POWERS OF THE SAPPHIRE
DOCTOR BOOMER
MOUSE TAILS
WILLOW AND ALBERT

Text copyright © 1969 Margaret J. Miller
Illustrations copyright © 1969 Charles Keeping

All rights reserved. No part of this book
may be reproduced in any manner without the
written permission of the publisher, except
in the case of a reviewer who may quote brief
passages for a review in a magazine or newspaper.

Published in the United States of America by
David White, Publishers
60 East 55th Street
New York, New York 10022

Library of Congress Catalog Card Number: 69-13470

The Stories

FOR VIOLET, WITH LOVE

Introduction

MOST of the tales in this book – English, Scottish, Irish and Welsh – belong to the fourteenth century, and all of them were popular in their day. I have chosen them from a host of others because they are particularly good stories to read. And I have tried to present them as *stories*, which means often that some of the detail and comment in the original versions has been omitted.

Henryson's fables with their homely humour show us animals who seem real and yet have something very human about them as well. Barbour's *The Battle of Bannockburn* is a splendid tale of war. The delicacy of *Sir Orfeo*, the magic enchantment of *The Children of Lir* and *The Dream of Macsen Wledig*, the noble deeds of the tales of Arthur, make these absorbing reading. It was difficult to decide which tale of Chaucer should be included. But *The Franklin's Tale* does show some outstanding sides of that many-sided man – well-drawn characters, good dialogue, and a shapely plot. *Adrian and Bardus* is one of the short tales which Gower told gracefully and neatly.

Before books were printed, stories were written down by hand. Very few people had the chance to read them. They were sung or told by minstrels who wandered from place to place. The author of *Sir Gawayn and the Green Knight* writes early in his tale: 'I shall tell it straightway as I heard it told in the dwellings of men.' One can easily imagine *Havelok the Dane* being told to a crowd in a market-place. And each time it was told, a tale might be changed a little in the telling, or altered by the scribe in the long, slow business of writing it down.

In 1476, a successful English merchant called William Caxton returned to England from Bruges. While he had been abroad he had learnt the craft of printing, which was becoming widely used in Europe because of the new methods which had recently been established in Germany. Caxton set up a printing press at Westminster in a house which became known as 'the house of the Red Pale', because of the sign above it. He was the first English printer, and Chaucer's book *The Canterbury Tales* was one of the first books he printed in England. Later he also printed Malory's *Morte d'Arthur*.

At the time when the stories in this book were first written down, there was no recognized standard English. People from one part of the country often could not understand people who came from another. You can read in the notes at the end of the book that Barbour wrote his *Bruce* in Lowland Scots, the author of *Sir Gawayn and the Green Knight* used the dialect of Cheshire and Lancashire, and the author of *Sir Orfeo* – according to some scholars – the dialect of south-western England. And you can see from the short extracts printed in the notes how very different one dialect was from another. It was through Caxton and his printing press that the dialect of London and south-east England, the dialect in which Chaucer and Gower wrote, became at last the English which most people wrote and spoke. Out of it grew the standard English that we know today. For Caxton and his successors could print hundreds of copies of a book where before only one copy at a time could be laboriously written out by hand. These books were much cheaper than the hand-written books and were available to many more people all over the country.

Before Caxton returned to England he had printed the first book in the English language, a popular French romance called the *Recuyell of the Histories of Troy*. 'Recuyell' means 'collection'. When he printed this book Caxton wrote:

> Therefore I have practised and learned at my great burden and expense to provide this said book in print after the manner and form as you may here see, and it is not written with pen and ink as other books be, to the end that every man may have them at once, for all the books of this story named the recule of the histories of Troy thus emprynted as you here see were begun in one day, and also finished in one day.

Three of the stories in this book I have retold from translations made by other authors. All the others I have translated myself from the originals. Here and there I have had to change words or add a few words for the sake of clarity, but I have kept as closely as possible to the spirit of each original. And where the author has used unusual but particularly expressive words I have not attempted to translate at all. Sir Bedivere says to the dying Arthur:

'Sir, I saw nothing but the waters wap and waves wan.'
What modern writer could improve upon that?

Robert Henryson

The Fox and the Wolf

ONCE upon a time there was a farmer. He had a plough and some oxen. And in the spring of the year he used to rise early and go out to plough his fields.

He would yoke up his oxen, cry 'Bless you!' to them, and start work.

As he ploughed he shouted to the oxen again.

'Ho there! Up and away now! Pull straight, my hearties!'

He prodded them with a stick to urge them on.

The oxen were not used to ploughing. They were young

and skittish. They began to frisk about and spoil the furrow.

Then the farmer got as mad as a March hare. He shouted. He flung his stick at the oxen. He even threw big stones at them.

'All right! The wolf shall have you all!' he yelled. 'I don't care!'

The wolf was nearer than the farmer knew. He and Lawrence the fox were skulking in a tangled thicket at the edge of the field. And they both heard what the farmer said.

Lawrence the fox laughed and laughed.

'It would do no harm to make that man stick to his promise,' he said.

'Yes,' said the wolf. 'I swear I'll make him keep it.'

Well, the oxen were better behaved after that. And as it was getting late, the farmer soon unyoked them and began to drive them home.

As he did so, who should come hirpling along but the wolf. He put himself in front of the oxen and got ready to speak. The farmer saw him and was filled with fear. He wanted to turn back with his beasts and avoid passing the wolf.

But the wolf spoke out.

'Where are you driving these oxen? What right have you to drive them? None of them belong to you.'

The farmer was more frightened than ever.

'Sir,' he said humbly, 'these oxen are all mine. Why should you stop me, then? I never did you any harm.'

'You say the oxen are yours,' answered the wolf. 'Have you forgotten that you gave them to me just now, when you were ploughing? "The wolf shall have you all!" That's what you told them.'

'Sir,' said the farmer, 'a man may say a thing in anger and then take it back when he has thought it over. Have you a witness who heard me promise? Did I put my promise down in writing?'

'Fie on the man who is not true to his word!' answered the
wolf. 'You promised, and that is that.'

'Where is your witness?' repeated the farmer.

'I have one, right enough,' said the wolf. 'Lawrence!
Come out of that copse and say what you heard and saw.'

Lawrence the fox came skulking, for he preferred to stay
hidden until darkness fell. And when the farmer saw him he
did not laugh, you may be sure.

'Now Lawrence,' said the wolf, 'I have called you as a
witness. What did this man promise me a little while ago?'

'Ah sir,' said the fox, 'I can't give you an answer to that
all at once. But if you both agree to do what I say, I'll try to
judge the case and please both of you.'

'Content!' said the wolf.

'And I,' added the farmer.

'Very well,' said the fox. 'Tell me what all the trouble's
about.'

'This man promised me his oxen,' said the wolf. 'You heard
it as clearly as I did, Lawrence. "The wolf shall have you
all!" he said.'

'But I didn't mean it,' protested the farmer. 'I never
intended to give my oxen to the wolf. I only said it because
I was angry.'

'Well, I will be judge,' said Lawrence. 'Swear to do what
I decide.'

The wolf stretched out his paw, the farmer his hand. And
they both swore to let the fox decide the case.

The fox took the farmer to one side and spoke to him
quietly.

'Don't make any mistake about this, my friend. The wolf
will make you give him every single one of your oxen.
However, I'd like to help you if I can.'

'Please do!'

'I can't do anything that's not right, of course. But look

here. You must have noticed that bribes – presents, you know – are often the best way of settling things.'

'How d'you mean?'

'You give somebody a hen and that saves you from losing an ox. That sort of thing.'

'I see,' said the farmer. 'Well, sir fox, you shall have six or seven of the very fattest hens I've got, if you'll only save my oxen for me. I care not how many hens I lose. Just leave me the cock, that's all.'

Lawrence the fox chuckled.

'Fine!' he said. 'If you give me those hens I'll put everything right for you.'

Having arranged to get the farmer's hens, Lawrence went off to the wolf. He got him away by himself in a patch of heather.

'You don't really mean to say you insist on having those oxen? You must be mad!'

'What d'you mean, "mad", Lawrence? You heard yourself the promise the farmer made when he was ploughing. That the wolf should have his oxen.'

'That's no reason why you should get them. He didn't mean it, you know. And as for me, I couldn't do any harm to a fine man like that.'

'What shall I do, then?'

'Listen. I've talked to the farmer and we've made this arrangement. If you'll let him off giving you the oxen he'll give you a cheese instead.'

'A *cheese*?'

'Mind you, you've never seen a cheese like this in the whole of your life. It's a summer cheese, fresh and beautiful. And heavy! It weighs a stone or more, the farmer says.'

'D'you mean to say,' said the wolf, 'that you advise me to let the farmer off his promise just for a cheese?'

'Certainly.'

'I can hardly bear to do it.'

'It's much the best thing for you.'

'All right,' said the wolf. 'I won't argue any more. But if you think I should give up all those oxen for one cheese – well, it must be a wonderful cheese. I should like to see it.'

'Come along then,' said the fox. 'The farmer told me where to find it.'

By now it was dark. The fox led the wolf through desolate woods, stealing from tree to tree, while the stars came out and the moon shone in the night sky.

All the time Lawrence was trying to think of some trick to cheat the wolf. Why had he promised him a cheese?

'Lawrence,' said the wolf, 'you're playing blindman's-buff with me. We seek all night and find nothing.'

But Lawrence had just thought of an idea. He was smiling softly to himself.

'We're almost at it, sir,' he said. 'Keep calm for a little longer. You shall see the cheese soon.'

Just then they came to a house. The moon was as full as a new penny, and it lit up the whole countryside. Near the house was a well with two buckets hanging in it. Our two fine fellows, the wolf and the fox, drew near the well.

Down at the bottom of the well shone the reflection of the moon.

'Now sir,' said Lawrence, 'you shall find that you can trust me. Just look down. Can't you see the cheese, as white and round as a turnip? The farmer hung it there so nobody could steal it.'

The wolf peered over the edge of the well.

'A cheese like the one you see hanging there,' went on the fox, 'would be a fit present for a lord. For a king, even!'

The wolf licked his lips.

'If I could have a cheese like that on dry land beside me,' he said, 'I'd let the farmer off his promise at once. His oxen

aren't worth a flea compared with that. Yes, there's the food for me!'

He licked his lips again.

'Lawrence,' he urged, 'jump into one of the buckets. I'll hold the other one while you go down.'

So Lawrence went down the well in a bucket, while the wolf stayed at the top.

'How are you getting on?' inquired the wolf after a time. 'When are you coming up with the cheese?'

'The cheese – is – so – huge,' panted Lawrence. 'I can't get a proper hold of it. It has dragged every single nail out of my toes.'

'What shall we do? I must have it.'

'Jump into the other bucket and come down and help me!'

Now Lawrence knew very well that when one of the well-buckets went down the other came up. And that is just what happened.

The wolf leapt lightly into the bucket. His weight made the other bucket rise, so the fox came rushing up as the wolf went down. This made the wolf very angry.

'I'm coming down to help you. Why are you hurrying away like that?'

'Sir,' said the fox, 'that's what life is like. As one man goes up in the world another goes down. Enjoy your cheese!'

Lawrence leapt on land as blithe as a bell, leaving the wolf up to his waist in water. Who pulled him out I do not know, for that is the end of the story.

Anonymous

Sir Orfeo

ONCE upon a time, in days of old, there was a king in England called Sir Orfeo. Orfeo was valiant and bold and courteous. And above all things he loved to play the harp. He played so skilfully that his hearers might well think they were listening to the harps of Paradise.

Sir Orfeo had a queen called Dame Herodis, the fairest and sweetest lady who had ever reigned in England.

One year, early in May, on a day that was warm and merry, Dame Herodis went into an orchard with two of her maidens. The rains of winter were over, every field was full of flowers, and every bough laden with blossom. Dame Herodis and her maidens sat down under a fruit tree to listen to the birds singing.

Soon the queen fell asleep, lying on the grass. Her maidens dared not waken her. They let her lie and take her rest.

Dame Herodis slept for a long time. But at last she woke, and immediately she began to scream terribly.

She scratched her face until it bled. She tore her rich robe. And all the time she went on screaming.

Her frightened maidens ran to the palace and spread word that the queen was going out of her mind.

Knights and ladies hurried to the orchard. They took the queen up in their arms and brought her to her bed in the palace. There they held her down, while all the time she cried out that she must be up and away.

When Orfeo heard this news he came to his lady and said with great pity:

'Dear love, what ails you? Why is your face so wan and your eyes so wild? I beg you, lady, cease this crying and tell me how I can help you.'

At last the queen lay still, weeping bitterly.

'My lord,' she sobbed, 'you and I must part. Tomorrow I shall have to leave you.'

'Then I am destroyed,' said Orfeo. 'Where must you go, and to whom? Wherever you go, I shall go too.'

'That cannot be,' replied Herodis. 'I will tell you why. As I lay and slept in our orchard this morning I had a dream. I dreamt that a king came riding up to me. A hundred knights rode beside him, and a hundred damsels in dresses white as milk, mounted on snow-white horses. The king wore a crown which was neither of silver nor of gold, but of some precious metal as bright as the sun. This fairy king made me ride beside him on a palfrey. He took me to his palace and showed me castles and towers, rivers and forests and flower-filled meadows. Then he brought me back to our orchard once more.'

'And then?' asked Orfeo.

'Then he said to me "Lady, tomorrow you must be here under this fruit tree. And then you shall go with us and live with us for evermore. Do not try to resist. Wherever you are we shall find you and take you away".'

'Woe is me!' cried Orfeo. 'I would rather die than lose my beloved wife. What shall I do? What shall I do?'

Orfeo asked each of his knights in turn to advise him. But none of them could think of any way to help.

The next morning Orfeo took a thousand knights with him, each one strongly and grimly armed. And with the queen he went to the fruit tree where she had fallen asleep the day before. Dame Herodis lay down on the grass and Orfeo spoke to his knights.

'Protect your queen well!'

'We would rather die than let her be taken from us,' they replied.

'We must watch carefully,' said Orfeo. 'We must not let the fairy king – where is she? Where is the queen?'

The knights looked under the tree where the queen had been a moment before. They looked about the orchard. There was no one there. The queen had been taken away from the very midst of them without their seeing it.

Then there was much weeping and woe among the knights and ladies of Orfeo's court. The king himself went to his room and grieved so sorely that he nearly died. But there was nothing to be done. Dame Herodis was gone.

At last Orfeo called together the chief men in the land.

'My lords,' he said, 'I shall leave my high steward here to rule my kingdom for me. And now that I have lost my queen I shall go into the wilderness and live in the woods with the wild beasts.'

The nobles wept and begged the king to stay. But they could not change his mind.

'Enough!' he said. 'It must be so.'

Wearing only the coat of a poor pilgrim, Orfeo took his harp and walked barefoot out of town. Through woods and over moors he went until he came to a wilderness. And there he dwelt, all alone.

He who had been a crowned king, owning castles and towers, rivers and forests and flowery meadows, had only the hard heath for his bed. In summer he lived on wild fruits and berries. In winter, on roots and grasses. His beard, black and rough, grew down to his waist. His only comfort was his harp.

He kept his harp in a hollow tree. And when the weather was fine he took it out and played on it.

The sound of the harp spread through the wood, and all the wild beasts that lived there followed the sound and drew close to Orfeo. Birds perched on branches near him, and birds and beasts together listened to the music until it came to an end.

Another thing happened to Orfeo. On hot days he saw the fairy king with his followers hunting all about him. With faint cries and with horns blowing they rode, and with barking hounds beside them. But he never saw them capture any beast. And when they went he knew not whither they had gone.

One day sixty ladies rode past him, each one graceful and gay as bird on bough. Each bore a falcon on her wrist as they rode hawking by a river. And each falcon slew its prey. Orfeo watched them and laughed.

'On my word this is fair sport,' said he. 'I will join them and seek out the wild birds – mallards, and herons, and cormorants.'

He drew nearer to one of the ladies, and suddenly he saw that it was his own queen, Dame Herodis. She saw him too, but neither spoke a word to the other. Tears fell from her eyes when she noticed his poverty and suffering. Then the other ladies made her ride away, leaving Orfeo alone.

'Alas!' he cried, 'my life has lasted too long, when I dare not speak a word to my wife nor she to me. I shall follow these ladies, even if it brings me to my death.'

So, taking his harp upon his back, Orfeo followed where the ladies led. Into a rocky passage they rode, and the king went after them.

When he had gone through the rock for three miles or more he came to a fair country, bright and green and flat. In the midst of this plain was a castle, wondrous high, with an outer wall of clear shining crystal.

There the ladies lighted. When they had gone in, Orfeo knocked at the gate and the porter came.

'What do you want here?'

'I am a minstrel. I should like to play to your lord, if he will allow me.'

The porter opened the gate and Orfeo went into the castle.

Within the castle Orfeo saw many people whom the fairy king had taken prisoner. They lay as though fast asleep, just as they had been brought from our world to the world of fairy. And among them was his own sweet wife Dame Herodis, sleeping beneath a fruit tree. He could tell her by her clothes.

Then Orfeo went into the great hall where the fairy king

sat on a throne with his queen beside him. He knelt down before the king and spoke.

'Good lord, would it please you to hear my minstrelsy?'

'What kind of man are you?' asked the king. 'You are brave indeed to come to this land without being sent for.'

'I am only a poor minstrel, sire. We are not always welcome I know, but we must offer to show our skill.'

'Then play to me.'

Orfeo sat down before the king. He set his merry-sounding harp in front of him, and he tuned it. And so blissful were the notes he made that everyone in the palace came to hear him. The king sat still and listened willingly. So too did the queen.

When Orfeo stopped playing the king spoke.

'Minstrel, I like your music well. Ask of me what you will, and I shall give it to you.'

'Then, good sir king, I beg you to give me that lovely lady who lies sleeping over there beneath an orchard tree.'

'Nay, minstrel, that would never do. You are shaggy, and black, and lean. While she – she is a beauty without flaw. You would make a wretched couple.'

'Gentle king, it would be more wretched to hear lies from your mouth. You promised me anything I asked for. You must keep to your word.'

'Take her by the hand, then, and go.'

Orfeo knelt down and thanked the king. He took Dame Herodis by the hand and led her out of the land of fairy.

When he reached his own city no man knew him. He left Herodis in a beggar's hut by the city gate, and, borrowing the beggar's cloak, he hung his harp on his back and went further into the town. Wherever he went men stared at him.

'Just look at that man's long hair!'

'His beard hangs right down to his knees!'

'He's like an old withered tree!'

As Orfeo walked along he met the steward, the man he had left in charge of his kingdom.

'Good steward,' he said, 'have mercy on me! I am a harper, poor and needy.'

'Then come with me,' said the steward. 'All harpers are welcome to me for the sake of my lord Sir Orfeo.'

The steward took Orfeo to the great hall of the castle. Many minstrels made music there while the feast went on. And Orfeo sat still and listened. At last it was his turn. He took his harp and began to play.

The music he made was so lovely that all men marvelled. And the steward recognized the harp.

'Minstrel, where did you get that harp? Tell me quickly!'

'Lord, far away from here I was crossing a wilderness. There in a dale I found a man all torn to pieces by wolves and lions. By his side lay this harp.'

'Woe is me!' said the steward. 'That was my lord Sir Orfeo. Alas that ever I was born, to hear that he has come to so vile a death!'

'Now steward,' said Orfeo, 'I know that you are a true man. I am Orfeo. I have brought my queen Herodis out of the land of fairy. She waits in a beggar's house in this very town. And for your loyalty you shall be king after me.'

The steward leapt to his feet. Over and over he threw the table. And then he knelt before Sir Orfeo. So did every lord in that hall. And they all cried out together:

'You are our lord, sir, and our king!'

So King Orfeo was crowned again with his queen Dame Herodis. For many long years they reigned together, and when they died the steward reigned after them.

Anonymous

Havelok the Dane · 1

LONG ago there was a very good king in England called Athelwold. Athelwold fell sick, and knew that he was going to die. His wife was dead and he had only one child, a baby daughter. When he felt death coming upon him he said to himself: How will my daughter fare now? She can neither speak nor walk. Who will look after her until she is ready to reign over England?

Athelwold sent for all his barons and earls from Roxburgh to Dover. And when they came he asked them who would best care for his daughter Goldborough. They replied that Earl Godrich of Cornwall was a true man, and that he could be trusted with Goldborough until she became queen.

Then the king made Earl Godrich swear on the Bible that he would look after Goldborough until she was ready to marry. He made him swear that he would give Goldborough to the tallest, handsomest and strongest man he could find, and that he would then give the kingdom into her keeping. And Earl Godrich swore.

Soon afterwards the king died and Godrich ruled the kingdom. He seized the whole of England and put knights he could trust into the castles. All England stood in awe of him. All England dreaded him as the beast fears the whip.

The king's daughter grew into a wise and lovely maiden. And when Earl Godrich heard men praise her he sighed and said to himself: Why should Goldborough be queen and lady over me? I have a fair son. He shall be king of England instead.

Godrich forgot his oath. He sent for Goldborough and put her in prison in Dover Castle on the seashore. She was poorly dressed, and none of her friends were allowed to come and see her in the castle.

Now we will leave Goldborough for the moment and go to Denmark where there was a king, strong and rich, called Birkabeyn.

Birkabeyn became ill. Neither gold nor silver nor any gift could save his life. He sent for his friend Godard and asked him to swear to take charge of his son and two daughters until his son Havelok could carry arms and be made king of Denmark.

Godard swore, but when the king died he imprisoned the children in a tower where they cried for hunger and cold.

Then Godard thought of a treacherous plan. He rode to the tower. And drawing out a knife he slew the king's two little daughters. He was about to slay Havelok too. But Havelok knelt down before Godard and said:

'Have mercy on me, lord. If you spare me I will leave Denmark today and never come back again.'

When that devil Godard heard this he was touched with some pity. He wished that Havelok were dead, but he did not want to slay him himself.

If I let him live he might do me much harm, he thought. And if he were dead my children could rule Denmark after me.

So he sent for a fisherman called Grim and promised him a great reward if he would take Havelok and drown him in the sea.

Grim took the child, bound him up with strong rope, put him in a dirty black bag and carried him to his cottage.

There he told his wife, Dame Leve, what he was going to do.

In the middle of the night Grim got up from his bed and dressed.

'Go and blow the fire and light a candle,' he said to Leve. 'I shall carry the boy to the sea and drown him there.'

Leve went to do as she was bid. Havelok was lying on the floor of the cottage, still tied up with rope. And all about him Leve saw a light shining, as brightly as though it were day. From his mouth came a ray of light like a sunbeam.

'What can this mean?' cried Leve. 'Grim! Rise up and see what you make of this light.'

Grim and Leve hurried to Havelok and untied his bonds. And as they did so they found a royal birth-mark on his right shoulder.

'Ah!' said Grim. 'This child shall one day be king of Denmark and of England too.'

Grim went down on his knees before Havelok and said:

'Lord, have mercy on us both. My wife and I will feed you and serve you until you are old enough to bear arms.'

Havelok was right glad at that.

'I am nearly dead for hunger,' he said.

'Then, lord, I shall bring you bread and cheese,' said Leve. 'And butter and milk, and pasties and cakes.'

She brought the food and Havelok ate hungrily and with good cheer.

The next day Grim began to think.

'If Godard finds out that this boy is alive,' he said, 'he will have us hanged. We had better fly from this land.'

So Grim sold all his corn, his sheep, his cattle, his horses and swine and bearded goats, the geese, and the hens in the yard. He painted his ship with tar, and stopped its seams with pitch. And he set sail with Havelok, Leve, his three sons and his two daughters.

When they were only a mile from the land a north wind

rose and blew them to England. There they landed near the River Humber, at the place which is now called Grimsby. And there Grim built a cottage for himself and his family.

Grim made a living by fishing both with net and with hook. He took many kinds of fish from the sea. He caught sturgeons, whales, turbot, salmon, seals and eels. He caught cod and porpoises, herring and mackerel, halibut, plaice and skate. He made baskets for himself and his sons, so that they could carry fish inland to sell.

Often he took his fish to the good town of Lincoln. And when he came home again he was happy, for he brought cakes, bags full of meal and corn, meat, hemp to make lines, and ropes for nets.

Thus for twelve winters Grim managed to live well. Now Havelok knew that Grim worked hard for a living while he himself stayed at home.

'I am not a boy any longer,' he said one day. 'And I eat more than Grim and his five children put together. To-morrow I will go out with a basket on my back and earn my food.'

Next day he set off with a basket heaped with fish. He could carry as much as four ordinary men. He sold the fish well, and brought money home. And so he went out, day after day.

But now a famine came, and Grim could not think how to feed his family. He gave no thought for his own sons; his only care was for Havelok. So he said to him:

'Havelok, dear son, this famine is so great that we may die of hunger. You had better go away to earn your meat. Go to Lincoln, for you know it well. But first I will make you a cloak out of my sail, to keep you from the cold.'

Grim took the shears down from a nail and cut up his sail to make Havelok a cloak. And Havelok put it on and went barefoot to Lincoln.

For two days he starved because he got no work. Then on the third day he heard a cry.

'Porters! Porters are needed here!'

Earl Godrich's cook Bertram was buying meat at the bridge, and wanted it carried to the castle. Havelok shoved nine or ten other lads out of the way, carried the meat to the castle, and was rewarded with a cake.

The next day he kept watch eagerly for the cook until he saw him on the bridge with a great quantity of fish lying beside him.

'Porters! Porters!' called Bertram.

Sixteen lads stood in Havelok's way. He pushed them back and leapt up to the cook. Then he took up very nearly a cartload of cuttlefish, salmon, plaice, lampreys and eels.

When he brought it to the castle the cook looked at him.

'Would you like to stay here?' he asked. 'I'll gladly feed you if you will work for me.'

'Give me enough to eat,' said Havelok, 'and I'll fetch water for you, blow the fire, break sticks, skin eels, wash dishes and do anything else you like.'

'I ask no more,' said Bertram. 'Sit down and I'll make you some broth.'

So Havelok stayed at the castle. He carried in water from the well and food from the market at the bridge. He brought in peat and wood for the fire. He worked as hard as a beast of burden all day, and yet he was always gay and cheerful. Well did he conceal his sorrow. Everyone loved him – knights and children, young and old. And the word went round about how tall Havelok was, and how strong, and how handsome.

Bertram bought him new clothes to replace his wretched cloak made out of Grim's sail. He bought him stockings and shoes. And when Havelok was properly dressed he looked like a king or an emperor. When men gathered at Lincoln for sports Havelok was the tallest by a head and shoulders. He could beat anyone at wrestling. And yet he was mild and kind.

Now it happened that parliament was meeting in the town, and at the same time many champions came to try their strength in games. All sorts of men gathered – farmers carrying their whips as though they had come straight from the plough, grooms who looked after horses, fair men and dark men, tall men and short.

On the ground lay a huge stone as heavy as an ox. The young men tried to lift it and throw it. The strongest man could scarcely lift it to the height of his knee. And he who could throw it an inch or more further than another was reckoned a champion, were he young or old.

Havelok had never seen stone-throwing like this. He was standing watching when his master the cook bade him try his hand at it. Havelok was afraid to disobey Bertram. So he picked up the stone. And at the first throw he threw it more than twelve feet further than anybody else.

The men in the crowd who were watching jostled one another and laughed.

'We'll do no more throwing!' they said. 'We can never beat that.'

A wonder like this could not be kept secret. Soon it was known all over the kingdom that Havelok had thrown the stone further than any of the other lads. In the hall at the castle knights spoke of Havelok's strength and might. And the news came to Earl Godrich.

Godrich, you remember, was ruling over England. He was keeping Goldborough, the dead king's daughter, a prisoner in Dover Castle. When Godrich heard about Havelok he said to himself:

'This boy will be a help to me. Now I can think of a way to get all England for myself and for my son when I die.'

2

GODRICH went on plotting how to keep England for himself and his son.

'Havelok shall marry Goldborough,' he thought. 'After all, I swore to King Athelwold that I would give her to the tallest, strongest and handsomest man I could find.'

Now when Godrich decided this he imagined that Havelok was a poor man's son. And he thought that if Goldborough married a servant boy she could not possibly become queen of England. But he suffered for his sins, as you shall hear.

Godrich sent for Goldborough to come to Lincoln. He had the church bells rung to welcome her, but there was treachery in his heart. He told her that he was going to marry her to the handsomest man alive. She said that she would wed no man, no matter how handsome, who was not a king, or a king's son.

'So you want to be queen over me?' said Godrich. 'I'll tell you you shall have a low fellow for a husband. You shall marry the servant who helps my cook.'

Next day Godrich sent for Havelok.

'Would you like to get married, lad?' he asked.

'Nay,' said Havelok. 'What should I do with a wife? I could not clothe her or feed her. I have no house nor cottage. All I own is an old white cloak. The very clothes I have on were given me by the cook my master.'

But though Goldborough cried and Havelok was unwilling, Godrich threatened them so much that they had to do his will. And so they were married.

Now what was Havelok to do? He saw that Godrich hated both him and his wife. And he feared that he might harm them. So he decided to take Goldborough back to the cottage of Grim the fisherman.

31

When he had journeyed there he found that Grim was dead. But his five children were all alive, and they welcomed Havelok and his wife with joy. They knelt down before him and said:

'Lord, stay here with us. We have houses, and cattle, and ships, gold and silver and many provisions that Grim left us. We have sheep as well, and swine. And all these things you shall share.'

So Havelok and Goldborough stayed, and a fine feast was made for their welcome. All the same Goldborough was sorrowful because she was married to a mere serving lad.

That night as she lay in bed beside Havelok she was wakened by a bright light like a blaze of fire. It was coming from Havelok's mouth. And at the same time she saw the royal birth-mark in the shape of a cross on his shoulder, and heard an angel's voice saying:

'Goldborough, be sorrowful no more. Havelok your husband is a king's son and king's heir. And one day he shall be king of Denmark and of England as well.'

This made Goldborough very happy. And soon Havelok wakened from his sleep and said:

'Wife, I have just had a wondrous dream.'

'Tell me.'

'I dreamt I was on a high hill in Denmark. And my arms were so long that I could encircle the whole of Denmark with them. All the strong castles fell on their knees to me, and their keys fell at my feet. And I dreamt another dream. I sped over the salt sea to England, taking many Danish men with me. And when I reached England I could hold the whole country in my hand. And then I gave it to you, Goldborough. What can this mean?'

'It means that you shall be king of Denmark and of England,' said Goldborough. 'But now do as I ask. Let us go at once to Denmark. I long to see the country which you shall rule as king. Ask Grim's sons to go with us, and let us set sail soon.'

So Havelok called together Grim's sons – Robert the Red, and William, and Hugh Raven. And he asked them to go with him to Denmark and help him to become king. They gladly agreed, and Havelok, with Goldborough and Grim's sons, set sail.

When they reached Denmark they went to the castle of a great earl called Ubbe, who had been a friend of Birkabeyn, Havelok's father. And Havelok begged Ubbe to let him live near him, and earn his livelihood by trading.

Ubbe looked at Havelok and saw how broad he was in the shoulders, how tall, and how strong.

'This man should be a knight,' he thought. 'It would be more seemly for him to wear a helm on his head and bear shield and spear than to live by trade.'

However he agreed to what Havelok asked. And he invited him and Goldborough to eat with him that day.

There was a great feast in Ubbe's hall. Roast swans were brought in, and cranes, venison and salmon, lampreys and sturgeon. There was spiced wine to drink – white wine and red, and plenty of it.

Ubbe thought Goldborough as fair as a flower. And he feared that men might attack Havelok to get his wife. So after the feast he sent Havelok and Goldborough and Grim's sons to stay with a friend of his called Bernard. And he asked Bernard to care for them well.

That night sixty thieves came to Bernard's house with long knives and drawn swords.

They shouted:

'Undo the door, Bernard, or we shall kill you!'

And they threw a great stone against the door and broke it.

Havelok saw this. He went to the door, pulled out the huge bar, and cast the door open wide.

33

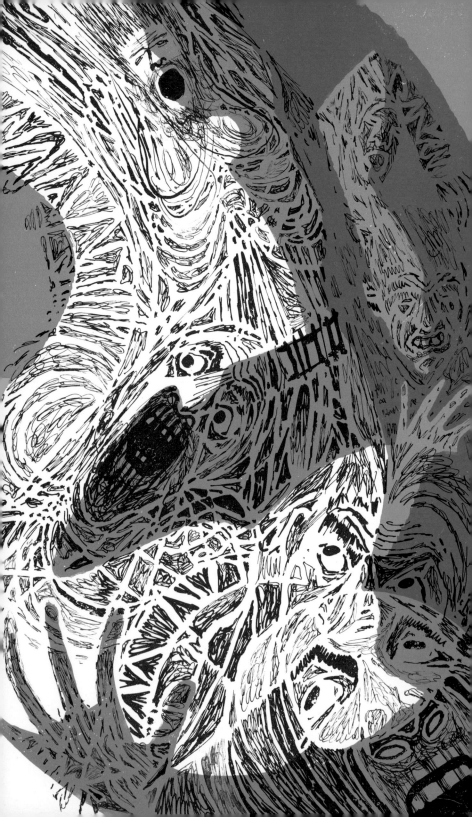

'Come on!' he cried. 'I am ready for you!'

The thieves rushed at Havelok. He heaved up the bar of the door and at one blow slew three of them. He clapped the fourth on the crown and gave the fifth a dint between the shoulders that sent him flying. The sixth tried to run away, but Havelok struck him in the neck with the bar and felled him to the earth. The seventh drew his sword, but Havelok smote him in the chest and killed him.

Then the thieves took counsel together and agreed to surround Havelok. They drew out swords and rushed at him as dogs do at a savage bear. Some attacked him with wood, some with stones. Some wounded him with their swords. Havelok laid about him furiously with the bar while the blood ran from his wounds. In a short time he had felled twenty men to the ground.

Hugh Raven heard the terrible din. He took an oar and a long knife and went to the place. And there he saw the thieves beating on Havelok as a smith beats on an anvil with his hammer.

'Robert! William!' he cried. 'Come quickly and help me drive these dogs away!'

Robert gripped a staff, William a great piece of wood. Bernard came with an axe. And after a fierce fight by the light of the moon every one of the sixty thieves was killed.

The next morning news of the fight came to Ubbe. Ubbe rode straight to Bernard's house and Bernard told him how the thieves came, and how Havelok fought them.

'That one man is worth a thousand men,' said Bernard. 'But he is badly wounded.'

Then Ubbe took Havelok and his wife Goldborough to a room high up in a tower. He said that they could stay there until Havelok's wounds were healed.

Ubbe's own room was next to the place where Havelok was. There was only a wall of firwood between. And the first night Havelok stayed there Ubbe woke up in the middle of the night. He saw a great light coming from the room where Havelok lay – a light as bright as daylight.

'Is Havelok revelling and drinking?' he said. 'I had better go and see.'

Ubbe went and peeped through a chink in the wall. He saw Havelok fast asleep beside Goldborough. And from his mouth came a shaft of light.

'What does this mean?' thought Ubbe.

He called his knights and bade them look. There was the gleam of light coming from Havelok's mouth like a sunbeam. And there on Havelok's right shoulder, brighter than gold, was the cross which showed them that he was a king. And they guessed that he was Birkabeyn's son, for he was as like Birkabeyn as a brother.

Now Havelok woke, and Ubbe and his knights fell on their knees and did him homage.

'You are very young, my lord,' said Ubbe. 'But you shall be king of Denmark.'

The next day Ubbe summoned earls and barons, clerks and knights, townspeople and country people, with their children and their wives. And he told them how Godard had treated Birkabeyn's children and how Grim had rescued Havelok and taken him to England.

'And now here stands your lord,' he said. 'Do him homage, all of you. I shall be the first.'

And once more Ubbe knelt down before Havelok and swore to serve him.

In the weeks that followed, men came from all over Denmark to swear loyalty to Havelok. And Ubbe dubbed him a knight, and he was made king of Denmark.

Ah, there was great joy then! There was wrestling, and throwing of the stone, and thrusting with sharp spears, and harping, and piping, and singing, and dinging on the drum.

There was baiting of bulls and boars. There was feasting. There was drinking.

Grim's sons – Robert the Red and William and Hugh Raven – were made barons and given land. And when the feasting was over Havelok sent a party of his knights out to find Godard and bring him bound before him. They made their way to a path along which Godard often rode to go hunting. Robert the Red, who was leading them, was the first to meet Godard.

'Beware, fellow!' he cried. 'You are to come with me to the king and be punished for your wicked deeds!'

There followed a fight between Havelok's followers and Godard's knights. Godard's knights fled, and Godard was bound and brought before Havelok.

Havelok ordered that his earls and barons and knights and townspeople should judge Godard, and they condemned him to be hanged. So died a false and treacherous man.

Then Havelok went with a strong army to England. He and Goldborough landed at Grimsby, where Grim had landed years before. When Godrich, the wicked earl of Cornwall, heard this he ordered every man who could wield arms to come to him at Lincoln.

The English dreaded Godrich as a horse dreads the spur. And they came to Lincoln on the appointed day, ready to fight against the Danes. Knights put on their bright coats of mail, placed their high helms on their heads, leapt on to their steeds and rode towards Grimsby.

Havelok with all his army came against the English. Bravely he laid about him with his sword, and Robert the Red and William, Hugh Raven and Ubbe fought fiercely too.

There was terrible slaughter on that battlefield. A thousand knights or more were slain on either side. Then Godrich began to attack the Danes like a lion. He felled them to the ground as a scythe cuts down grass, and nobody could stand against the dints of his sword.

When Havelok saw this he came galloping up on his horse, calling loudly:

'If you yield, Godrich, I will forgive you the wrong you have done, because you are so brave a knight.'

'I will never yield!' cried Godrich, and gripping his sword he hewed at Havelok and cleft his shield. Havelok drew his own sword and smote Godrich to the earth. But Godrich started up and hit Havelok so hard on the shoulder that he cut loose many rings of his coat of mail and wounded him deeply.

Then Havelok slashed with his sword and cut off Godrich's right hand. He took him by the neck and had him bound in steel fetters. And he sent him to Goldborough, to be cared for until he came to trial.

Now the English knew that Goldborough was the rightful heir to the kingdom. And when Havelok had sent six earls to fetch her from Grimsby, her people came to do her homage.

'Lady,' they said, 'we know well that Athelwold was king of this land, and that you are his heir. Have mercy on us, and never again will we rise against you.'

After this Godrich was tried and condemned to death, and all the English swore that they would be loyal to Havelok.

Havelok did not forget the kindness of Bertram, Earl Godrich's cook. He made him Earl of Cornwall instead of Godrich, presented him with all the land that Godrich had held, and gave him one of Grim's daughters for his wife.

Then Havelok went to London to be crowned king of England. And for sixty years he ruled England happily with his queen, the fair Goldborough.

Now you have heard the story of Havelok the Dane.

Robert Henryson

The Lion and the Mouse

ONE day a lion lay under a tree in a beautiful forest, warming himself in the sun. He was worn out from hunting, and all he wanted was to rest.

Some mice who had a burrow close by came scuttering out, playful and gay. They tripped along until they reached the lion. Then they began scrambling over his body.

The lion lay so still that the mice were not afraid. To and fro they went across him. Up, down and over. And then back again.

Some of them plucked at his whiskers. Some scrabbled on

his face with their little claws. They squeaked with joy as they played about.

Now all this time the lion had been asleep. But at last he woke up. He waited a moment. He noticed that one particular mouse was the leader in the game. Then suddenly he put out his paw and caught her.

She gave a squeak of terror. The other mice, frightened to death, stopped frisking and ran away and hid.

The captured mouse started crying and moaning.

'Oh, how I wish I had never come here! How I wish I'd never come!'

At last she spoke to the lion.

'Sir, I am a miserable prisoner. I have behaved very badly. Please tell me quickly – are you going to kill me or let me go?'

'Impudent wretch!' answered the lion. 'You seemed to think you had the right to trip about all over me. Had you forgotten that I am the king of beasts?'

'I know that. But you lay so still.'

'Humph!'

'You see it was like this,' the mouse continued. 'My friends and I had had plenty to eat. We hadn't a care in the world. It is spring, as you can see for yourself, sir. The boughs are laden with blossom, and – '

'Go on.'

'Because it is spring we felt like dancing. And there you were, lying so quiet. We thought you were dead. Really we did. Otherwise we would never have danced on top of you.'

'That is no excuse,' said the lion. 'Even if I had been dead and stuffed with straw you shouldn't have danced on me. You have shamed and dishonoured me. And for that you shall die.'

Still held fast in the lion's paws, the mouse began to plead and beg for her life.

'Sir, I know that I ought to die. I should never, never

have danced on you like that. But since you are the king of beasts the noblest thing you could do would be to show mercy.'

The lion's paw closed a little tighter. The mouse went on talking as fast as she could.

'What honour will it bring you to put me to death? A strong lion can kill and eat a thousand mice with no trouble at all. All the animals in the forest admire you. But will they admire you so much if you kill a mouse who can't defend herself? A mouse who has asked you to spare her life?'

The lion was listening. The mouse took heart.

'Besides, sir, you are a king, a noble animal. You are used to delicious food. It is not fitting that you should soil your teeth and lips with my blood. It – it would be harmful to your stomach.'

The mouse thought she felt the lion's paw unclose slightly. She hurried on.

'Mouse meat is indigestible. Especially to a lion who has been used to feeding on fine venison. And one last thing.'

Calling up all her courage, the mouse finished her speech.

'I know my life is worth little, sir. My death will mean nothing. But if I live, I may one day be able to help you. You never know. Sometimes a man of small importance has rescued a great lord from misfortune. One day that may happen to you.'

The lion had listened carefully. He had thought over everything the mouse said.

'Very well,' he growled. 'I will let you go.'

He opened his paw and the mouse fell on to the leaf-strewn ground of the forest. When she got her breath back she knelt down and held up her paws.

'May you be well rewarded, kind sir!'

Then, still trembling after her fright, she scampered to her burrow.

When the mouse was gone, the lion returned to his hunting. He lived by killing and eating other beasts, both tame and wild. And he caused such trouble in the countryside that the men who dwelt in those parts decided that they must try to capture him.

To do this, they wove a strong net. After that they tied the net with coarse rope to the trees on either side of a forest path. They knew the lion often went there.

Next, the men who were going to hunt the lion spread themselves out in a long line in the wood.

'Halloo!'

They blew their hunting horns and called up their dogs. The pack of dogs yelped and barked.

The sound of the hunt filled the forest. The lion fled from it. And running through a thicket he plunged headlong into the net.

His head and legs were entangled. His strength helped him not at all. There was nothing he could do.

He wallowed and rolled, roaring hideously. He stretched out to this side and that, seeking freedom. The more he flung about, the worse entangled he became. Now the ropes of the net were so tightly twisted about him that he lost hope.

Lying still, he moaned to himself.

'Miserable, miserable creature that I am! Every beast in the forest used to fear me, but who could fear me now? I see only one future before me. I shall have to lie here in this net until the hunters come to kill me.'

There was no answer. Only the rustle of the leaves of the forest and the sound of the horns and the hounds coming nearer, nearer.

'There is nobody to help me,' moaned the lion. 'Nobody to break the net and let me out of this prison. Nobody! Nobody!'

But he was wrong. By wonderful good fortune the little

mouse whom he had captured and let go was in the forest near by. She heard the lion moaning.

'The king of beasts is in danger,' she said to herself. 'And I would be very ungrateful not to repay his kindness.'

There was no time to lose. The hounds were barking loudly. The huntsmen were crashing through the trees. The mouse scampered off to her burrow and gave the alarm.

'Help, comrades, help! The king of beasts needs us!'

Scrabbling along as quickly as they could, the mice obeyed her call. Bustling and rustling among the forest leaves, they reached the lion where he lay in his net.

'Now,' said the leading mouse, 'this is the lion who let me go free when he might have killed me. If we don't save him the hunters will take him. Help me to do one good turn for another. Set him free quickly. Quickly!'

'We will! We will!' cried the other mice.

'There is no time to be lost!'

The mice knew this. They could hear the hunt loud with the sound of horns and the dogs' barking, coming through the forest.

'Work away! Work away, brothers!'

The teeth of the mice were as sharp as knives. They ran about among the tough ropes of the net, some on top, some underneath. They gnawed and gnawed until the ropes snapped.

'Halloo!'

Just one more rope. Ten mice attacked it at once, and the lion started up, free of danger.

Quickly he thanked the mice and darted off into the forest. When the hunt reached the spot a moment later, he was gone.

And the mouse who had saved him, snug in her burrow, knew that he would be glad, very glad, that he had listened to her when she pleaded for her life.

from the Mabinogion

The Dream of Macsen Wledig

ONCE upon a time there was an emperor of Rome whose name was Macsen Wledig. He was very handsome and very wise.

One morning early, Macsen Wledig set out with his friends and servants to go hunting. All morning they hunted, until the sun was high above their heads in the heavens. And then it grew very hot, and Macsen Wledig lay down to sleep.

His chamberlains propped their shields about him on the shafts of their spears, to screen him from the sun. They put a golden shield beneath his head. And in this way Macsen slept.

As soon as he was asleep he began to dream. In his dream he went along a river valley until he came to a mountain which seemed to him the highest mountain in the world. Yes, he thought the mountain was as high as the sky itself.

In his dream he crossed the mountain, and now, on the far side of it, he was travelling across a fair plain. He saw wide rivers flowing from the mountain towards the sea. And he journeyed until he came to the mouth of one of these great rivers.

At the mouth of the river was a mighty city. And in the city stood a castle with many towers of different colours. And on the river a fleet was waiting – the biggest fleet ever seen by man.

In the fleet Macsen Wledig saw a ship, bigger and fairer than all the other ships there. Its planks were of gold and silver, and a bridge of walrus-ivory stretched from the ship to the land.

Macsen Wledig crossed the bridge and stepped on to the ship. A sail was hoisted, and away went the ship over the ocean. At last it reached an island, the fairest in the world.

Macsen crossed the island from one sea's edge to the other. And he reached a country of valleys and cliffs and towering rocks – a harsh country whose like he had never seen. A mountain he saw, and a river flowing toward the sea.

We are still talking about Macsen's dream, remember. Well, in his dream he saw a great castle at the river mouth, the fairest ever seen by man. The gate of the castle was open, and he went in.

Inside the castle Macsen saw a fair hall. Its roof and doors were of gold, and its walls of glittering stones. He saw golden couches in the hall, and silver tables. And on a couch he saw two red-haired young men playing a game, with a silver board and golden pieces.

By a pillar in the hall he saw a grey-haired man seated in a chair of ivory. A golden board was before him, and he was carving pieces for a game like the game the youths were playing.

And as Macsen stepped forward in his dream he saw a maiden sitting before him in a golden chair. She was dressed in white silk with golden clasps, and on her head was a gold band set with rubies and pearls. She was the fairest maiden ever seen by man.

And the maiden rose from the chair of gold to meet

Macsen, and he threw his arms round her neck, and –

But then he heard the whining of dogs straining at the leash, and the clash of shields striking against each other, and spear shafts clattering, and the stamping of horses. And Macsen Wledig awoke from his dream.

His servants saw him wake.

'Lord,' said one, 'it is past time for you to take your meat.'

And then Macsen the emperor mounted his horse, the saddest man that ever was, and made his way towards Rome.

What could he do? The only thing he wanted to do was to sleep. For when he slept he saw in his dreams the woman he loved best. And when he awoke he cared for nothing, because he knew not where in the world to find her.

One day his chief lord spoke to him.

'Lord, your men are all speaking ill of you.'

'Why do they speak ill of me?' asked Macsen.

'Because you give them no leadership these days, such as men expect from their lord.'

'Then call the wise men of Rome about me, and I will tell them why I am sad.'

So the wise men of Rome came to the emperor, and he spoke to them, and told them about his dreams. And they advised him. 'Lord, this is our counsel. Send messengers to the three divisions of the earth, to seek your dream. And then, since good news may one day come to you, you can hope and not be sad.'

'I will do that,' said Macsen Wledig.

So the messengers went forth and journeyed till the end of the year, wandering the world and looking for the country of Macsen's dream. But when they came back at the end of the year they knew nothing more than on the day they set out. And the emperor grieved that he should hear no news of the lady he loved best.

Then the chief lord spoke to Macsen.

'Lord, go forth to hunt the way you saw yourself go in your dream.'

So the emperor went hunting and came to a river.

'It was here that I was when I began to dream!' said he. 'And from here I was journeying westwards.'

Then thirteen men set forth as messengers of Macsen Wledig. And presently they saw before them a huge mountain which seemed to them as high as the sky. They crossed it, and they saw a fair plain with wide rivers flowing towards the sea.

'Lo,' they said to one another, 'here is the land our lord saw.'

They journeyed to the mouth of one of the rivers, and at the mouth was a mighty city. In the city stood a castle with towers of different colours. And on the river, a fleet, and one ship bigger than all the rest.

'Lo once more,' they said, 'the dream our lord saw.'

In that great ship they sailed over the sea and came to the island of Britain. And they crossed the island till they came to a rugged land.

'Lo once more, the valleys and cliffs and towering rocks our lord saw.'

They pressed forward until they could see a mountain.

'Lo,' they said, 'the land our lord saw in his sleep.'

They saw the river, and the castle at the river mouth. The gate of the castle was open and they went in, and into the hall.

'Lo, the hall our lord saw in his sleep.'

They saw the two youths playing a game, and the grey-haired man in the ivory chair. And – yes, there in a chair of gold was the fairest maiden in all the world!

The messengers went down on their knees.

'All hail, empress of Rome!'

'Why do you mock me?' asked the maiden.

49   D

'This is no mockery, lady. The emperor of Rome has seen you in his sleep. Life means nothing to him without you. Will you come with us to be made empress in Rome, or shall the emperor come here for you?'

'If the emperor loves me,' said the maiden, 'then let him come here to fetch me.'

By day and by night the messengers sped back, changing horses when their steeds failed them. And when they reached Rome they came before the emperor.

'We will be your guide, lord,' they said. 'We will lead you by sea and by land to the lady whom you love the best.'

Straightway Macsen Wledig set out with his horse, and with the messengers to guide him. Over land and sea they went towards the island of Britain.

And when Macsen came to the rugged land with its valleys and cliffs and its towering rocks he recognized it at once. And there was the castle.

'See yonder,' he said, 'the castle in which I saw the lady I love best.'

Macsen went into the castle, and into the hall. He saw the two youths playing a game. He saw a grey-haired man sitting in a chair of ivory, carving pieces for the game.

And there, sitting in a golden chair, was the maiden he had seen in his sleep.

Macsen Wledig knelt down.

'Empress of Rome,' he said, 'all hail!'

And that is how the emperor Macsen Wledig found his bride.

The Children of Lir

LIR was one of five kings who ruled Ireland long ago. Another of these kings was Bov the Red. Bov had two fair daughters called Eva and Aoife. And Lir fell in love with Eva and married her.

Lir and Eva had three sons and a daughter. Their names were Hugh and Conn, Fiachra and Fionuala. And then, alas, Eva died.

Because he was lonely Lir left his own home at the Hill of the White Field and went to stay at the palace of Bov the Red. And Bov said he would give him Eva's sister Aoife for his wife.

So Lir married Aoife, and at first she was good to his children. But Lir loved them so dearly that Aoife became jealous. At last she thought of a black and evil deed.

One fine morning when Lir was away on a journey she told the children that she was going to take them to visit their grandfather, Bov the Red. Fionuala feared her stepmother and did not want to go. But Aoife had her horses and chariot put ready and made the children travel with her away from the Hill of the White Field.

Westward they went till they came to the shores of Loch Derryvaragh. There they made a halt.

'Go and swim in the loch, children,' said Aoife.

The children were glad to do this. And while they were in the water Aoife worked her witchcraft upon them.

'Fly and float with the wild birds, children of Lir!' she cried. 'Never come back to your father again!'

Fionuala glanced down at her reflection in the still waters of the loch. Her neck was long, and her golden hair and rich clothes had turned to snow-white feathers. Aoife had changed her into a swan. Looking at her brothers she saw that they were swans too.

But Fionuala could still speak. 'Evil is your deed, Aoife,' she said. 'Tell us at least whether our doom can have an end.'

'Hush and listen!' chanted Aoife. 'None will release you till the Woman of the South weds the Man from the North!'

'And how long will that be?'

'Three hundred years shall you stay on the waters of Derryvaragh, three hundred years upon the stormy straits of Moyle, and three hundred years where the Western Ocean rolls in upon the shore.'

'Nine hundred years! Alas! Alas!'

'I leave you two things,' said Aoife. 'You may keep your human speech, and you shall sing sad music lovelier than any music in all the world.'

Then Aoife got into her chariot and drove to the palace of Bov the Red.

'Where are Lir's children?' asked Bov.

'I knew if I brought them you would keep them and never let them go,' said Aoife.

Bov thought this strange. And he sent messengers secretly to the Hill of the White Field where Lir had returned from his journey.

'Why have you come?' asked Lir.

'To bring your children to Bov the Red.'

'I thought Aoife had taken them.'

Then Lir was afraid. He set out westward until he reached the shores of Loch Derryvaragh.

'Father! Father!' cried Fionuala when she saw his chariot. 'We are your four children! Aoife was jealous of us, so she has turned us into swans.'

At that Lir was nearly mad with grief.

'But we have the gift of music,' said Fionuala. 'Stay by the shore here tonight and we will sing to you.'

So Lir listened the whole night through to the singing of the swans. All the high sorrows of the world were in that music, and it plunged Lir in dreams which he could never tell.

Next day Lir went on to the palace of Bov the Red and told him the story.

'You shall be punished for ever!' cried Bov to Aoife. And he smote Aoife with a wand so that she became a demon of the air and flew shrieking from the hall.

The swans stayed on the waters of Loch Derryvaragh. And while they were there there was a great peace and sweetness and gentleness in the land. People came from all parts of Ireland to listen to their music, and when they heard it they felt their ills no more.

But one day Fionuala said to her brothers:

'Do you remember our doom, my dear ones? Three hundred years we have lived on this loch. Now we must go for three hundred years to the stormy straits of Moyle.'

Her brothers were sad, for they feared the angry waves of the cold northern sea.

Early next day the four swans went to the side of the loch to bid farewell to Bov the Red and their father Lir. Fionuala sang them her last lament.

Then she and her brothers rose high in the air and flew northwards.

They came to a wide coast beset with black rocks and great

precipices. On it beat the salt, bitter waves of an angry sea – cold, grey and misty.

'Must we live here for three hundred years, sister?' asked Conn.

'Yes,' said Fionuala. 'That is our doom.'

It was winter when the four white swans came to the straits of Moyle. Day after day the waves dashed upon the rocks. The air was so thick with snow they could scarcely see one another.

One night there was a terrible tempest.

'We may be driven apart by the wind, brothers,' said Fionuala. 'Let us fix a place where we shall meet when the storm is over.'

'The Seal Rock,' said Conn.

'Yes,' said Hugh and Fiachra. This was a rock which they all knew well.

Throughout that black night the waves roared upon the coast with a deafening noise. Thunder bellowed from the sky, and lightning was all the light the swans had. They were blown apart by the violence of the storm, and when the wind fell at dawn Fionuala found herself alone upon the ocean swell not far from the Seal Rock.

'Where is Hugh? Where is Conn?' she lamented. 'Where is my little Fiachra?'

Eagerly she watched the tossing waters until at last she saw Conn coming towards her, his head drooping and his feathers disarranged. Then came Fiachra, cold and wet and faint, and with the speech frozen in him so that not a word he said could be understood. And last of all came Hugh with his feathers unruffled because he had found shelter.

Fionuala put Fiachra under her breast and Conn under her right wing and Hugh under her left wing.

'O children of Lir, we shall have many nights like this one,' she sighed.

So they lived on in that place of storms until one day Fionuala said:

'Brothers, today we must fly to the west.'

'To the west? Why, Fionuala?' asked Hugh.

'Have you forgotten the spell?'

'No!' cried the brothers.

And they all chanted:

'Three hundred years upon the loch of Derryvaragh,
Three hundred years upon the stormy straits of Moyle,
Three hundred years where the Western Ocean rolls
                                       in upon the shore.'

Then the swans rose up wheeling in the air and flew westwards across Ireland.

They suffered much from cold and tempest in the waters of the Western Sea. But as time went on they knew that the day was drawing near when they would be free from the spell.

And at last the three hundred years was over.

'Come, brothers,' said Fionuala, 'let us fly to the Hill of the White Fields to see our father Lir.'

So together with eager hearts they flew on and on until they came to the place where they had spent their carefree childhood years. And what did they find? Green grassy mounds where once there had been houses and palaces. Withered bushes, and forests of nettles. They drew together and lamented aloud, for they knew that old times had passed away in Ireland, and they were lonely in a land of strangers.

Sad and bewildered, the children of Lir flew back to the shores of the Western Ocean.

Now it was the time when holy Patrick came into Ireland and preached the faith of one God. And a follower of Patrick, a hermit, had built himself a little church of stone close to the place where the swans lived. He spent his time in preaching and prayer.

The swans heard him chanting his service and went to listen. When the hermit came out from his church he spoke to them and they told him their story. And he in turn told them about St Patrick and how he had taught the people of Ireland about Christianity.

'Let us sing, brothers. Let us sing to the glory of God,' said Fionuala.

And the four swans sang a solemn, sweet, slow song in adoration of the High King of Heaven and Earth.

Now it came about that a princess in the south of Ireland was going to marry a chief in the north. And she asked for only one wedding gift – the four singing swans. The chief's men rode to the seashore to take the swans away.

'We should go gladly, brothers,' said Fionuala when she heard why they had come. 'Remember what Aoife said. "When the Woman of the South weds the Man from the North." The time of our release is near.'

The hermit followed the swan children all the way to the palace of the princess. And there he saw a strange and terrible sight.

As the swans were led before the princess, behold! their white feathers dropped away, leaving four withered old creatures more wrinkled and shrunken than anyone there had seen before. They were so old that they were at the point of death.

The hermit knelt beside them.

'Good hermit,' murmured Fionuala.

'Yes?'

'Lay us all together in one grave. Put Conn at my right hand and Hugh at my left. And put Fiachra before me. That is how I used to shelter them on the straits of Moyle.'

The hermit did as Fionuala asked. And he remembered the swan children of Lir and their wonderful singing to the end of his days.

from the Mabinogion

The First Great Deed of Peredur

PEREDUR was the seventh son of Efrawg, a mighty earl in the north. Efrawg was a great fighter. He went often to the wars; and at last he was slain, both he and his six sons.

Peredur's mother was wise. She did not want her seventh son to be slain. So she left the parts where most men dwelt and went with Peredur to a wilderness. She took with her only women and boys, and such men as had no skill in war.

Never a one dared mention horses or arms before Peredur, in case he should set his heart on these things. But every day the boy went into the forest to play. And he loved to throw darts cut from a holly bush.

One day Peredur saw a flock of goats belonging to his mother. Two hinds were standing near the goats. And Peredur could not understand why these two had no horns, while all the others had horns on their heads.

'I know,' he said to himself. 'These two have been running wild for a long time, and so they have lost their horns. I will see to it that they do not stray again.'

Peredur was very strong, and a fast runner. And although the goats were swift and wayward he drove them with the hinds all the way to the shelter at the far end of the forest. Then he went home.

'Mother,' he said, 'I have seen a strange thing.'

'And what is that, my son?'

'Two of your goats have run wild and lost their horns. I drove them into a shelter so that they should not run wild again. But it was a hard thing to do.'

Then all the servants who waited on Peredur's mother went to the shelter to look. And when they saw the goats and hinds they were amazed that Peredur had been strong enough and swift enough to drive them in.

Another day when Peredur was playing in the forest with his mother beside him, he saw three knights riding along a bridle path.

'Mother,' he said, 'what are those men over there?'

Now Peredur's mother did not want her son to become a knight and go to war. So she said:

'They are angels, my son.'

'I will be an angel and go with them, then,' said Peredur. And he went along the path to meet the knights.

One of the knights was called Owein. And Owein called to Peredur.

'Say, friend, have you seen a knight go past here lately?'

'A knight? I do not know what a knight is.'

'I am a knight,' said Owein.

'Then,' said Peredur, 'if you will answer some questions, I will tell you what you want to know.'

'Gladly,' said Owein.

'What is that?' asked Peredur, pointing to Owein's saddle.

'A saddle,' said Owein.

'And that?'

'A bridle.'

'And this?'

'The crupper.'

Peredur asked all about Owein's armour and his harness. And Owein told him what everything was, and how it was used.

'Now keep on as you are going,' said Peredur. 'I have seen

the knight you are looking for, going that way. And I too will follow you as a knight as soon as I can.'

Then Peredur went back to where his mother waited with her servants.

'Mother,' he said, 'those men were not angels. They were knights.'

Peredur's mother turned pale, and fell swooning to the ground.

While her servants attended to her, Peredur went to where the horses were kept. These horses were used to carry firewood, and to bring food and drink from far away to the wilderness. Peredur chose what he thought was the best horse there, though it was only a wan, piebald, bony nag. And he pressed a basket on to its back for a saddle. And then with willow withes he made a sort of harness, like that which he had seen on Owein's horse.

Peredur mounted the horse and went back to his mother. And when she saw him she knew what was in his mind.

'Are you really going?' she said.

'Yes.'

'Then let me advise you before you set out.'

'Speak quickly. I am waiting.'

'Go to King Arthur's court. There you will find the best men, and the most generous, and the bravest.'

'Very well.'

'Whenever you see a church, say a prayer. If you see meat and drink, and if you need it, take it yourself if no one offers it to you. If you hear cries, ride towards them, especially if the cries be a woman's. If you see a fair jewel, take it and give it to another. If you see a fair lady, be courteous to her.'

So Peredur went on his way, with a handful of holly darts in his hand. For two days and two nights he travelled through desert and wilderness, without food or drink.

At last he came to a great desolate forest. And deep in the

forest he saw a clearing, like a field. And in the clearing he could see a tent.

Peredur thought that the tent was a church. So, remembering what his mother said, he recited a prayer. Then he rode up to the tent. The door was open, and near it stood a chair made of gold, and in the chair sat a lovely auburn-haired maiden. About her forehead was a band of gold with sparkling stones in it. And on one of her fingers she wore a thick gold ring.

Peredur leapt from his horse and went inside the tent. The maiden welcomed him, and at the back of the tent he saw a table with wine, and bread, and meat.

Peredur spoke to the maiden.

'My mother bade me to take meat and drink wherever I saw it.'

'Go to the table then, chieftain,' said the maiden. 'Eat, and be welcome.'

So Peredur went to the table, and he took half the food and drink for himself and left half for the maiden.

After this he went again to the maiden.

'My mother bade me take a fair jewel if I saw one.'

'Take it and welcome, friend,' said she.

Peredur took the gold ring from her finger. Then he knelt down and kissed the maiden, and afterwards he rode away.

Peredur went on his way to Arthur's court. But before he reached the court another knight came there. He gave a gold ring to the man at the entrance to hold his horse. And he went on to the hall where Arthur sat at meat with his knights. Guinevere was there with her maidens, and a chamberlain was pouring out wine for Guinevere from a goblet.

The knight took the goblet and emptied the wine over Guinevere's face, and gave Guinevere a great box on the ear.

'Now,' said he, 'if any one wishes to fight with me for this goblet and avenge this insult to Guinevere, let him follow me to the meadow beyond the castle. I will be waiting for him.'

Then all the knights there hung their heads lest they should be asked to fight. For they thought that surely no man would do such a thing unless he had some magic and enchantment to prevent anyone from harming him.

When the knight had left the hall, lo, Peredur came riding in. There he was on his wan, piebald, bony nag, with strange, badly-made trappings upon it. A sorry figure he was in that distinguished court.

A tall knight called Cei was standing in the middle of the hall floor.

'Say, thou tall man,' cried Peredur, 'where is Arthur?'

'What have you to do with Arthur?' said Cei.

'My mother told me to come to Arthur to be made a knight.'

'By my faith,' said Cei, 'on a strange horse you have come to Arthur, and with strange arms.'

Then the other knights saw Peredur, and they started to make fun of him and to throw sticks at him.

'Look at his saddle. It's only an old basket.'

'His harness is made of willow withes!'

'And such a horse. A half-starved nag!'

'Tall man,' said Peredur to Cei, 'I asked you to tell me where Arthur is.'

'Stop this babble,' said Cei. 'Go after the knight who rode out to the meadow just now. Take the goblet away from him, and overthrow him and take his horse and arms. Then you shall be made a knight.'

'Tall man,' said Peredur, 'I will do that.'

And he turned his horse round and rode out to the meadow.

When he reached the meadow, the knight was riding his horse about there, very proud and mighty.

'Say,' he called to Peredur, 'did you see any knight from Arthur's court coming after me?'

'The tall man,' said Peredur, 'told me to come myself. He bade me overthrow you, and take the goblet and your horse and arms.'

'Enough,' said the knight. 'Go back to the court and tell Arthur or some other knight to come and joust with me. And he had better come quickly, or I will not wait for him.'

'You can take your choice,' said Peredur. 'I will have the horse and the arms and the goblet whether you give me leave or no.'

Then the knight was very angry. He bore down on Peredur and dealt him a mighty blow between his neck and his shoulder.

'If that is your game,' said Peredur, 'I can play it too.'

And he aimed at the knight with a sharp-pointed dart and hit him so that he fell stone-dead to the ground.

In Arthur's hall the knights were talking among one another. Owein, the knight whom Peredur had met in the wood, was there.

'Faith,' said Owein to Cei, 'it was an ill thing to send that fool after the knight. One of two things will have happened. Either he has been overthrown or he has been slain. I shall go and see what has become of him.'

Then Owein went to the meadow. And when he got there, Peredur was dragging the dead knight behind him all along the meadow.

'Wait, chieftain,' said Owein, 'I will take off his armour.'

'Surely this iron suit will never come off him,' said Peredur. 'It is a part of him.'

'You shall see,' said Owein. And he took the armour off the knight.

'Here friend,' said he. 'Here are arms for you, and a horse better than the one you ride. Take them thankfully and come with me to Arthur, and you shall be made a knight.'

'Not I,' said Peredur. 'But do you take the goblet from me to Guinevere. And tell Arthur that wherever I go, I will be his man. And if I can do him good service, I shall.'

Then Owein went back to the court and told what had happened. And Peredur went on his way. And thereafter he did many many great deeds.

John Barbour

The Battle of Bannockburn

WHEN it was daylight the Scotsmen devoutly heard mass. Then they ate and got ready. And when they were all gathered in battle order with their broad banners flying King Robert the Bruce made several men knights, as is usual in warfare. He made Walter Stewart a knight, and James of Douglas, and other excellent men. When this was done they went forth in good array and took their places on the plain. Many a brave hardy man was there.

Opposite them they could see the Englishmen in their companies, shining as brightly as angels. They were not spread out like the Scots, but were drawn up closely. Whether it was from fear I know not. In any case they were drawn up closely, except for the vanguard who were assembled separately and were making ready for battle.

Many a glittering shield, much bright, polished armour, many a man of great valour and many gaily coloured banners could be seen among the English host.

When the King of England, King Edward the Second, saw the Scotsmen take the field on foot, he marvelled.

'What? Will yonder Scots fight?' he said.

'Yes, surely sir,' said Sir Ingram Umphraville, one of his knights. 'Now I see the most amazing sight that ever I saw – these Scotsmen prepared to give battle against the great might of England.'

'Wondrous indeed,' said the king.

E

'But if you will take my advice you shall easily beat them. All of a sudden, make a retreat with your forces and your banners till we get past our tents. As soon as you do that, the Scots will scatter in spite of anything their leaders can say. They will be hoping for plunder. Then, when we see them scattered, let us prick on them boldly, and we shall easily have them.'

'On my word,' said the king, 'I will never do that. No man shall say that I retreated from such a rabble as I see over there.'

After this the Scotsmen knelt down to pray to God to help them in that fight. When the English king saw this he exclaimed:

'Yon folk are kneeling to ask mercy.'

Sir Ingram said: 'You say truth. They are asking for mercy, but not from you. They are begging God to forgive them for their sins. I tell you one thing certainly. Those men will win all or die. Fear of death will never make them flee.'

'Be it so,' said the king. 'We shall prove it without delay.'

He ordered the trumpeters to sound the assembly, and with the king leading the Englishmen advanced. They galloped along, spurring their horses. And when the two hosts met, men might hear the clashing of spears from far away.

At that meeting many steeds were stabbed, and galloped and reeled about wildly. Men dinged upon one another with sharp axes and spears. Some fell, and had no strength to rise again.

The Scots pressed on to overthrow their foes, refusing no pain or peril.

Then one of the chief Scotsmen, the Earl of Murray, led his men to the thick of the fight, where there was a great crowding of men and banners. The English spurred at them as though they would ride right over the earl and his company. But the Scots stood sturdily, and laid many a good man low. Fallen men were trampled underfoot. Blood burst through breastplates and streamed to the ground.

The Earl of Murray and his men were outnumbered by ten to one, or more. But little by little they gained ground,

until they were swallowed up in the vast host as though plunged into the sea. The English saw how bravely they fought, and pressed them with all their might.

Men battled with bright swords, with axes, with spears, with maces and with knives. The grass grew red with blood. The clash of weapons upon armour was heard, knights and horses tumbled to the earth, and rich garments were trodden into the mud.

For a long time the fighting went on without any noise of shouting. There was only the sound of groans, and of blows which struck fire from armour as a flint does from steel.

The arrows flew thickly in a hideous shower, and where they hit they left their mark, you may be sure. The English archers shot so fast that they put the Scots in great peril. King Robert saw this. And he ordered his marshal, Sir Robert of Keith, to lead five hundred horsemen against the archers and attack them with spears.

Sir Robert rode down upon them so fiercely that they all scattered. Scottish archers saw them driven back and became daring. They shot eagerly among the English knights, slaying many.

When King Robert saw how well his men bore themselves in the fight he was blithe and merry.

'Be bold and daring, my lords,' he said to his leaders. 'Our men are fighting so fiercely that if our foes are pressed a little harder you shall see them overthrown.'

Then the Scots laid on with all their might and main, like madmen. And the English stood sturdily against them. There was such throwing and thrusting of spears, such striking of weapons on armour, such groaning and shouting of war-cries, that it was hideous to hear.

Anyone who saw Sir Walter Stewart and his troop and the good Douglas, another brave man, would say they were worthy of all honour. The noble Earl of Murray and his men gave such great blows and fought so fast in that battle that they made their foes give way.

Bravely the Scots shouted their war-cries:

'On them! On them! On them! They are falling back!'

With that the Scots attacked so hard and their archers shot among the English so stoutly that the English were in a worse plight than before.

While the fighting was going on, the camp followers had been left in a park to keep guard over the provisions. And now they chose one of their number to be captain of them all. They tied sheets on to poles and spears to take the place of banners. And they said that they would go and see the fight and help their lords.

When they were all gathered together there were fifteen thousand of them and more. And off they went in a crowd with their banners, like strong fighting men.

They marched to where they could see the battle, and then all at once they cried out:

'On them! On them boldly!'

They were still some way from the battlefield. And when the English, who were getting the worst of it, saw such a company coming towards them, they thought as many more men were joining the fight as were already fighting. And even the best and bravest man in that host wished he could leave the field.

King Robert saw by their faltering that they were near defeat. And shouting his war-cry he pressed upon them with his men. The English gave ground more and more. Some of them fled. But the braver men thought shame to fly, and fought on under great difficulty.

When the King of England saw his men fleeing he was so discouraged that he and all his company, five hundred well-armed men, took flight and rode off to Stirling Castle.

One of the King of England's knights, Sir Giles de

Argentine, saw his master go. And he galloped after him.

'Sir,' he said, 'if you are leaving like this, I bid you good day! For myself I will turn again. I never fled yet, and I choose to stay here and die rather than flee shamefully.'

Then he turned his horse and rode back. And like a man who fears nothing he spurred towards the company of Sir Edward Bruce, brother of King Robert.

'Argentine!' he shouted.

He was met by so many spears that he and his horse were brought to the ground, and he was slain. A great pity it was, for he was one of the best knights of his day.

After the king had fled, no other Englishman dared stay upon that field. They scattered in all directions. Many of them fled to the River Forth and were drowned there. Bannockburn itself was so full of drowned horses and men that a man might cross over it without getting wet.

When the camp followers saw that the day was won they ran among the English and slew men who could not escape. On the one hand these men had their foes, and on the other Bannockburn, deep and muddy. So some were slain and some were drowned.

There were thirty thousand English killed or drowned in this great battle. Some were taken prisoner and others escaped.

So many fled to nearby Stirling Castle that the rocks on which the castle stood were quite hidden by the crowd of men seeking safety.

When the battlefield was bare of Englishmen the Scots took for themselves any plunder they could find. And many a man was made mighty by the riches he got there. Then King Robert the Bruce and all his company were joyful and blithe and merry for the good fortune they had had in the battle. And they took their way to their quarters to rest. For they were weary.

Robert Henryson

The Country Mouse and the Town Mouse

ONCE upon a time there were two mice. They were sisters, and loved one another dearly. The elder mouse lived in a town, the other in the country not far away.

The country mouse lived now under bushes, now under briars, and now in the corn. Like an outlaw she lived, and got what she could by hunting.

In the winter the country mouse suffered from hunger, and cold, and great distress. The town mouse was much respected, and was free to go wherever she liked. She could always get herself cheese from the box or meal from the chest.

One day when this older mouse was feeling well-fed and lusty she thought of her sister in the country. She longed to know how she was, and to see what sort of life she was leading. So she took a staff in her hand, left the town, and began walking over hill and dale to seek her sister.

Over moss and moor she walked, over banks and through bushes. And presently she began to run, crying out:

'Come out to me, my own dear sister! Cry "Peep!" just once and then I will know where you are!'

The country mouse heard her, and guessed who it was by the sound of her voice. She came out at once.

If only you could have seen the joy when those two sisters met! They laughed, they cried, they kissed, they hugged each other. They went on like this until the first excitement was over. Then side by side they went into the country mouse's home.

A very simple dwelling it was. Just some moss and fern put together and reached by a small entrance under a stone. There was no fire, no brightly burning candle. Those who live by stealing like the country mouse love not the light.

When the mice were safely inside the younger sister went to her larder and brought out nuts and peas. The town mouse started to nibble, but after a few minutes she burst out:

'Sister, do you eat this sort of thing every day?'

'Why not? It's excellent food, isn't it?'

'No, by my soul. I think it's disgusting.'

'All the more shame to you, madam,' said the country mouse. 'I live in poverty as our mother did before us. There's nothing wrong with it.'

'Well, you'll have to excuse me, sister,' said the town mouse. 'This rough food will never agree with me. My stomach is used to tender meat.'

'Really?'

'Yes, sometimes I eat as well as any lord. I can't chew these withered peas and nuts. They'll break my teeth.'

'Well, well, sister, if you could be satisfied with this sort of thing you could stay here a year if you liked. At any rate it's friendly and cheerful. Good cheer and simple dishes are better than roasted ox and bad temper.'

But the town mouse could not be cheerful. Though her sister brought her every dainty she could think of, she kept on frowning. At last she said, half mockingly:

'Sister, this royal feast of yours may do for a country mouse. It won't do for me. Now listen. Leave this burrow and come to my place. The scraps from my table are better than your whole meal. I have plenty of safe holes. I'm not a bit afraid of cats or traps.'

'Very well,' said the country mouse. And off they went.

Through grass and corn they crept, and under bushes, always stealthily. The elder mouse went in front as guide. The younger followed her. They travelled by night and slept by day and reached the town early one morning before the lark had begun to sing.

The town mouse led her sister into a fine house, and straight to a larder where there was plenty of food. Cheese and butter were on the shelves, and meat and fish, both fresh and salt. On the floor were sacks of malt and meal.

'Is this better than your funny little nest?' asked the town mouse laughingly.

'Yes my dear. But how long will it last?'

'Why for ever, and longer.'

'Then you are lucky,' said the country mouse.

The town mouse brought out other dainties. A plate of groats, a dish full of meal, bannocks, white bread, and a white candle which she stole from a box.

So they made merry till they could eat no more. And from time to time they cried out 'Merry Christmas!' for it was as good as a Christmas feast.

But their joy did not last long. In the middle of all the fun the butler came with his bunch of keys, opened the door, and found them at dinner.

You can well imagine that they didn't wait to wipe their mouths. It was a race to see who could escape the fastest. The town mouse knew of a hole and popped into it. Her sister had no hole to hide in. It was pitiful to see that wretched mouse. She fell down in a faint, half dead with fear.

But luckily the butler was too busy to stay. He had no time to chase the mice out. He went away, leaving the door wide open. The town mouse saw him go. Out of her hole she rushed, crying aloud:

'How are you, sister? Cry "Peep!" wherever you are!'

The country mouse was lying full length on the ground, trembling from head to foot. When her sister found her in such a state she began to cry for very pity. Then she tried to comfort her with honey-sweet words.

'Why do you lie like this? Get up, dear sister. Come and eat again. The danger is over.'

'I cannot eat,' the country mouse answered sadly. 'I'm much too frightened. I would rather starve on thin broth and gnaw peas and beans than feast in fear like this.'

All the same, the town mouse managed to persuade her sister to get up. Down they sat at the table again. But they had only taken a few mouthfuls when in came Gilbert the cat.

The town mouse flew to her hole like fire on flint. And the cat took the country mouse by the back.

To and fro he tossed her, and up and down. Sometimes he let her run under the straw on the floor. Sometimes he teased her by pretending to close his eyes. He went on tormenting the wretched mouse until by good luck she managed to creep between the wall and a piece of boarding.

She scrambled up behind the board to be out of Gilbert's reach. Then she clung there by her claws till he went away disappointed. How thankful she was! She leapt down and called to her sister.

'Farewell, sister! I want no more of your sort of feasting! You can never eat without worry. That cruel beast nearly had me.'

'But – '

'Once I get back to my own home I won't leave it again.'

With that the country mouse said goodbye and left. Through cornfields and valleys and moors she made her way, thankful to be free.

At last she reached her little home. As warm as wool it was, however humble. And after all, it was well stuffed with beans and nuts and peas and rye and wheat. Yes, she had plenty to eat, and that in peace and quiet. And she never again went to share her sister's feast.

John Gower

Adrian and Bardus

THIS is a story about an ungrateful man.

Once upon a time a great lord of Rome called Adrian went hunting in a wood. And suddenly, while his mind was set on hunting, as ill luck would have it he fell into a deep pit.

None of Adrian's men were near him at the time. Nobody knew what had happened to him. So there at the bottom of the pit he lay all day long, calling and crying for help.

Towards evening it happened that a poor man called Bardus came walking by with his ass. He had gathered a bundle of green sticks and dry sticks to sell. This was his only livelihood, and he had put the bundle on his ass's back, meaning to go with it to town.

He lingered a moment by the pit in order to tie up the sticks more firmly. And as he did so he heard a voice crying faintly. Bardus knelt down and put his ear to the edge of the pit. Yes, it was a man's voice.

'Help! Help! I am Adrian, and I will give half my goods to anyone who helps me!'

Half his goods! That was something which Bardus would gladly win. So he called down to the lord who was in the pit.

'If I save you, how can I be sure that I shall get the reward you promise?'

The voice from the bottom of the pit answered.

'By heaven and by all the gods, I mean what I say. You shall have my goods, if you get me out of here.'

'Very well. I will.'

Bardus unloaded the sticks from his ass's back. And he let the cord which had tied them down into the pit, with a staff fastened on at the end.

'Take a hold of that, and I'll pull you up!'

But it happened that an ape had fallen into the pit as well as Adrian. And when the cord was lowered the ape skipped up to it and clasped it in both his arms.

Bardus and his ass pulled on the rope and up it came. When Bardus saw the ape, however, he thought the fairies had been playing tricks on him. And he was sore afraid.

Then he heard Adrian crying and praying for help again. And once more he cast the cord into the pit. When it came up this time a great serpent was wound round it. Surely this was a dream? But once more he heard the voice crying and he answered it.

'What manner of man are you? Tell me, for heaven's sake!'

'What man? Why, the same who promised you half his goods if you will only save me.'

'Then I'll try again. I'll try for the third time.'

Bardus threw the rope into the pit. And this time Adrian took hold of it and called to Bardus to haul up. Bardus and his ass together pulled and pulled. And thus they drew Adrian up to the firm ground at the side of the pit.

What happened then? Adrian never even stopped to say 'Thank you'. He set out at once for Rome, leaving poor Bardus without his reward.

Well, Bardus put his bundle of sticks on his ass again, and went home. When he got there he told his wife what had happened. But Adrian was a great lord. Bardus did not dare to go and ask him to give what he had promised.

The next day, Bardus went out as usual with his ass and his rope to gather wood. And when he came to the place where he meant to collect sticks, lo and behold, there was the ape. He had collected a great pile of wood and put it all ready for Bardus.

You can imagine how pleased Bardus was as he fastened up his bundle. And day after day the ape helped him like this, making sure that he had plenty of wood.

Then another day as Bardus drew towards the forest he saw the great ghastly serpent, the one he had rescued from the pit, gliding towards him. She came up to him and made him a sort of bow as best she could. Next, she opened her mouth and dropped from it a stone brighter than crystal.

She laid the stone at Bardus' feet and glided quickly away so that he should not be frightened.

Poor Bardus was delighted. Thanking God in his heart, he picked up the stone. And it came to his mind that the two beasts had repaid him, while Adrian, for whom he had done so much, had not.

Bardus went home and showed the stone to his wife. And they both agreed that he should sell it. So he went straight off to a jeweller and was given gold in payment.

Full of joy, Bardus went back to his wife. And when he took the gold out of his purse to show it to her, he found that the stone was there too.

This was extraordinary.

'Look wife,' said Bardus. 'Here's the gold. And yet – here's the stone as well.'

'Then you didn't sell it?'

'Indeed I did. I took it to a merchant and he gave me this gold for it. I tell you what I'll do. Tomorrow I'll take it and sell it somewhere else. And if it creeps into my purse again, why then I can truly say that that's the sort of stone it is.'

The next day came, and Bardus went off to find somewhere else to sell the stone. He sold it to another merchant, and again when he got home the stone was in his purse as well as the gold.

This happened everywhere he went. Several times he sold the stone. And yet, when he opened his purse at home, there was the stone and the gold too.

Such things cannot be kept secret. People in Rome began to talk about the wonderful stone. And at last the Emperor Justinian sent for Bardus and asked him about it.

Well, Bardus told him the whole story. He told him how the serpent and the ape, though they had made no promise, had well repaid him. And he told him how Adrian had promised him half his goods and had given him nothing.

The Emperor said that he would put this right. Adrian was brought before a court of judgment. And the court decided that Bardus should have half of Adrian's goods.

The tale of Adrian and Bardus is told to this day to remind us that it is a shame to be ungrateful to our fellow men.

Anonymous

Sir Gawayn and the Green Knight

1 THE GREEN KNIGHT'S BARGAIN

ONE Christmas time King Arthur was at Camelot with a company of fair ladies and knights of the Round Table. For fifteen days they feasted, held tournaments, and jousted jollily. By day a cheerful din filled the halls. By night there was dancing.

On New Year's Day, when the service in chapel was over, New Year's gifts were given in hall. Then everyone washed and went to table. Lovely Guinevere sat in the middle under a silken canopy embroidered with the best gems that pennies could buy.

The first course was brought in with a cracking of trumpets. Pipes warbled, kettledrums sounded. And, at that moment, in at the hall door rode a terrible knight.

He was so huge that he seemed half giant, half man. And strangest of all, his body, his clothes and the horse he rode upon were bright green.

His coat and his mantle were green, and his spurs and his stirrups. His horse's green mane was wound about with threads of gold. Golden bells hung on its green tail. The knight's green beard was as big as a bush. He wore no armour and carried no spear. But in one hand he held a holly branch, the greenest thing to be found when the woods are bare. And in the other he gripped a mighty axe.

The knight rode straight up to the high table where Arthur sat.

'Where is the governor of this gang?' he shouted. 'I wish to speak to him.'

He looked the knights over, swaggering up and down on his horse.

Then Arthur, who was afraid of nothing, saluted him and spoke.

'I am Arthur, the head of this hall. Light graciously down and stay, I beg you.'

'No, I must not stay. But if you are as bold as men say, you will do as I ask.'

'If you crave battle, my knights are ready.'

'I want no battle. There is not a man here to match me. The knights on these benches are only beardless children. No, I ask in this court a Christmas game.'

'A Christmas game?'

'Is any man bold enough to deal me a blow with this axe of mine? Then, a year from now I shall return the blow and he must not resist. Come, is any so bold?'

There was silence in the hall. The knight rolled his red eyes about, knit his bristling green eyebrows, and swept his beard from side to side as he looked this way and that.

'What,' he said, 'is this really King Arthur's Court? Where are your pride and your conquests now, your fierceness, your wrath, your great words? Why, the renown of the Round Table has been overturned with a word of one man's speech! Yes, you all cower for dread without a blow shown!'

Arthur stormed with anger.

'By heaven, knight,' he said, 'you have asked a foolish thing. Here, give me your axe. You shall have your blow.'

But Gawayn, who was sitting by Guinevere, bowed to the king and spoke.

'Uncle – I beg you let the challenge be mine.'

'Take the axe then, nephew, and strike bravely.'

As Gawayn went up to the green knight, the stranger spoke to him.

'First, sir knight, tell me your name.'

'I am called Gawayn.'

'I am honoured to take the blow from your hand, Sir Gawayn. Now, what is our agreement?'

'I shall give you a blow. And in a year's time you will repay it.'

'Well said. And remember – you must seek me yourself until you find me.'

'Where do you live?' asked Gawayn. 'I know you not, sir knight, neither your court, nor your name.'

'I will tell you when you have smitten me. Come, take that grim axe. Let me see what a knock you can give.'

The green knight knelt on the ground and bowed his head till his long hair fell forward, leaving his neck bare. Gawayn gripped the axe and raised it above his head. Then he let it light down on the naked flesh. The blade of the bright steel bit the ground, and the green knight's head was cut clean off.

But the knight neither faltered nor fell. He jumped to his feet, his legs quite steady. He caught up his green head, turned to his horse, and seized the bridle. He stepped into the stirrup and mounted. Then, while he held the head in his hand, his mouth spoke:

'Gawayn, I charge you to go next New Year's morn to the green chapel to receive a blow like the one you gave me here. I am the knight of the green chapel. Ask, and you shall find me. Many men know me.'

The knight turned and rode out of the hall door with his head in his hand. The fire of flint flew from the hooves of his steed. And nobody there knew what land he went to, or from what land he had come.

Christmas passed, and the seasons in their turn. The cold shrank away, the clouds lifted, and the ground and the trees wore green raiment. Birds bustled to build, and sang for joy of soft summer that followed the spring. The harvest hastened on, and hardened the seed. And next the grass, which had been green, grew grey once more.

Thus the year passed in many yesterdays, and winter came again to the world.

Now Gawayn must go on his troublesome journey. Early one morning he asked for his arms and prepared himself for his task. And when he was ready he mounted upon his horse Gringolet and bade farewell to King Arthur and his knights.

'My lord Arthur, I must take my leave and go to seek the green chapel and the green knight. Farewell to you, Sir Percival, and to you, Sir Kay, to Launcelot and Lionel and Lucan the good, Sir Bors and Sir Bedivere, and Mador de la Port!'

'Farewell, Gawayn! God speed you!' cried the knights.

Sir Gawayn rode away through the realm. And as he went he questioned men that he met.

'Ho there, woodcutter! Can you tell me where I can find a green knight and a green chapel?'

'No, sir knight, I have never heard of them.'

Sir Gawayn came upon many perils. He warred with dragons and with wolves, with trolls who dwelt in craggy places, with bulls and bears, with giants and boars. And wherever he travelled he asked the same question.

'Ho there, shepherd, can you tell me where the green chapel lies? Have you heard of the green knight?'

'Alas no, gentle sir knight.'

Nearly slain with the sleet Gawayn slept in his armour among naked rocks. Cold streams ran clattering down from the heights, and hung above his head in hard icicles.

Thus in peril and pain Gawayn travelled until Christmas

Eve. Then he rode into a deep forest with high hills on either side. Here there were tangled hazel and hawthorn trees, and huge, aged oaks all rough with ragged moss. On the bare boughs were many sad birds, piteously piping for pain of the cold.

'Oh Lord,' sighed Gawayn, 'pray give me some harbour where I may hear mass and praise thee this Christmas.'

Suddenly he saw a shimmering and a shining through the trees.

'Jesus be thanked!' he cried. 'It is a castle! Now grant me good lodging. On, Gringolet!'

Gawayn urged his horse forward with his gilt spurs until he reached the castle. Its towers and pinnacles were as white and new as though they were cut out of paper. There was a moat round about it, and the drawbridge was pulled up.

Gawayn called out, and a porter appeared and greeted him.

'Good Sir,' said Gawayn, 'would you go to the lord of this house and ask if I may have lodging here?'

'Yea, by St Peter,' said the porter. 'And I am sure, sir knight, that you will be welcome to stay as long as you please.'

Then the drawbridge was let down, and people from the castle came out to receive the knight. The broad gate was set wide open, and Gawayn rode into the courtyard.

His horse was taken away to the stable and knights and squires escorted him to the hall, where a fire burned brightly. The lord of the castle came from his room to greet Gawayn.

'Sir, you are welcome!' he cried. 'Treat everything here as your own.'

This lord was a huge knight. His red beard was bright and broad. His speech was free and his face fierce as fire. Gawayn thought he seemed well suited to rule over knights in a strong castle.

Servants waited on Gawayn. They led him to a room with a noble bed in it. The curtains of the bed were pure silk hemmed with clear gold. Tapestries hung on the walls. The servants took off the knight's armour and brought him rich robes to wear.

Then a chair by the chimney in the hall was set with cushions for the weary knight. And he sat on that splendid seat and warmed himself, and was filled with good cheer.

A table was put up on trestles and covered with a clean white cloth. Many kinds of food and wine were brought in, and the lord of the castle asked where Gawayn came from. When he learned Gawayn's name and that he hailed from Arthur's court he laughed loudly for joy. And every knight there was glad that Gawayn, so courteous and so noble, had come to them that Christmas.

When dinner was done the bells rang for chapel, and Gawayn went to the service with the rest. Afterwards the lady of the castle came to the hall. Her complexion was fresh and rosy; round her bright throat she wore clear pearls. Gawayn thought her even lovelier than Queen Guinevere.

So the company talked and laughed by the fireside, while servants brought them spices and wine. And at last the lord called for lights to light them to bed.

Christmas Day was a day of feasting. There was meat, there was mirth, there was much joy. Yes, much joy was made that day and the next, and the third followed after as full of delight. The joy of St John's day was gentle to hear, and it was the last day of sport in that hall.

There were guests to go on the grey morn. So they stayed up and drank wine, and danced, and sang carols. At last, when it was late, they parted. And the lord of the castle took Gawayn to his room.

'And now, sir knight,' said the lord, 'stay longer, I beg you. My castle is honoured while you dwell here.'

'I thank you, my lord, but I cannot stay.'

'Have you left the court for some deed of valour? Tell me, why are you travelling thus at Christmas time?'

'Sir, I have been summoned to seek a certain place. And I know not where in the whole world to go to find it. Have you ever heard tell of the green chapel? And of a green knight who lives there? I must be there on New Year's Day, and I have barely three days left.'

'The green chapel?' laughed the lord. 'Let the matter grieve you no more, Sir Gawayn. It is only two miles from this very place. So you must rest here until New Year's Day, and one of my servants shall set you on the way to it.'

'Then the end of my quest is in sight,' said Gawayn. 'Thank you, my lord. I will stay as you wish.'

At that the lord became very merry.

'Now, sir knight,' he cried, 'would you do something for me if I asked you?'

'Certainly,' said Gawayn. 'While I stay in your house I will do your bidding.'

'You have travelled far,' said the lord, 'and since you have been here you have stayed up late. You need rest and sleep. Lie in bed at your ease tomorrow until meal-time. You can go to your meat when you like, with my wife, and she will sit with you. And I shall rise early and go hunting.'

'As you wish.'

'Besides, let us make a bargain. Whatever I win in the wood shall be yours. And whatever you gain, you shall give to me. Good sir, let us swap so. Come, swear it.'

'I willingly swear,' said Gawayn.

So they drank and they dallied and they revelled. And at last they took leave of one another courteously. And servants led each knight to bed by the light of gleaming torches.

But before they parted, the lord of the castle repeated the bargain they had made.

'Remember, sir knight. What I win in the wood shall be yours. And what you win in the castle shall be mine.'

2 SIR GAWAYN FINDS THE GREEN CHAPEL

BEFORE daybreak next morning people were astir in the castle. Guests who had to go called to their grooms to saddle their horses. Then they seized their bridles, leapt up lightly, and rode away.

The lord of the castle was one of the earliest. Dressed for riding, with his knights about him, he made for the hunting fields to the sound of the bugle.

The hounds bayed, the wild beasts quaked for fear, and with a great din the deer were driven into the deepest glades.

'Hay!' and 'Ware!' cried the huntsmen.

At every turn in the wood arrows slipped and slanted and rushed along. And as the arrows flew, deer fell, and bled and died.

Hounds leapt upon them and hunters galloped after, blowing their loud horns with a cracking cry like rocks toppling to the ground.

So the lord passed the hours hunting the deer, while at the castle Gawayn lay still in his curtained bed until the daylight gleamed on the walls.

Then, as he dozed, he heard a little din at the door of his room.

He heaved his head out of the clothes, cast up a corner of the curtain, and saw that it was the lady.

'Good morrow, Sir Gawayn,' she said.

'Good morrow, fair lady.'

'Sir Gawayn, I have come to beg you to stay here. Do not go to look for the green chapel.'

'Ah, but I must go.'

'Stay here for my sake.'

'I have given my word. I must not break it.'

'I shall hope to change your mind,' said the lady. 'Your honour and your courtliness are praised wherever you ride. I have got Sir Gawayn here. I should like to keep him. Meanwhile, let us talk together.'

'My gracious lady,' said Gawayn, 'I am your servant and your knight, to talk when you will, and do your wishes.'

'But I doubt after all if you are Gawayn,' said the lady.

'Why, lady?'

'Gawayn is known for courtesy through the world. And surely he would kiss his lady.'

'Let it be as you wish,' said Gawayn.

The lady bent down and kissed Gawayn lightly, and he kissed her.

'Now dress speedily,' she said. 'And we shall make merry till the moon rises. Then my lord will be coming home from the wood with the hunters.'

Meanwhile the lord went on with his hunting. And by the time the sun set he had slain a wondrous quantity of deer. Then with loud notes sounding on the horns the huntsmen rode homewards. By the time daylight was done they were all in the castle, and the lord was greeting Gawayn by the bright fire.

'Ho! Bring the venison into the hall!' called the lord. 'Now, Sir Gawayn, what do you think of this? Have I won praise for my day's work?'

'My lord, this is the fairest hunting I have seen these seven years in the season of winter.'

'It is all yours, Gawayn. By our bargain you can claim it as your own.'

'And you shall have what I won today in the castle.'

Gawayn took the lord in his arms and kissed him.

'Gramercy!' cried the lord. 'Your winnings are good. It would be better still if you would tell me how you won this prize.'

'That was not the agreement,' answered Gawayn. 'Ask me no more.'

Next day when the cock had crowed and cackled only three times the lord and his knights leapt from their beds. They went to the chapel, they ate a hasty meal, and again they rode with hounds and horns to the wood.

The hounds were called to search by the side of a marsh. Forty hounds at once got on the track, and there was such a babel and din of gathered hounds that the rocks rang all round about. To a hill by a cliff where rough fallen rocks were scattered the hounds ran to the finding. They nosed about the cliff and the hill, for they knew well that a beast was somewhere there. Then the huntsmen beat on the bushes and bade the beast come forth. And out rushed a huge boar.

He grunted grimly and charged forward. He stood at bay and hurt some of the hounds so that they piteously yawled and yelled.

Huntsmen quailed and withdrew in fear. But the lord on a light horse galloped after the boar, boldly blowing his bugle.

So they passed the day with hunting, while Gawayn lay at home in his bed and heard again a voice at his door.

'Sir Gawayn, once more I beg you to stay. Do not go to seek the green chapel.'

'I must go, lady.'

'Then I will give you one more kiss.'

The lord's hunting was going well. At last the boar was so exhausted it could run no more. It stood near a stream with a bank at its back and began to scrape the ground, foaming at the mouth.

The lord leapt down from his horse. He drew out a bright sword and bigly strode forth. The boar rushed out upon him until they were both struggling in the stream. The boar had the worse of it, for the man marked well, and drove his sword into the beast's throat. Then, as the snarling boar floated downstream, the hounds finished him off.

When the lord rode home the boar's great head was carried before him, and its carcase was slung on a strong pole.

'Sir Gawayn!' cried the lord. 'See what I have brought you!'

Gawayn handled the huge head.

'In truth, my lord,' he said, 'it is a terrible beast. Now I shall give you what I got today.'

And he put his arms round the lord's neck and kissed him.

'Tomorrow I must go to the green chapel,' he said.

'As I am a true man,' answered the lord, 'I give you my word that you shall reach the green chapel by dawn on New Year's Day. Take your ease here for one day more. I shall go hunting again and give you my winnings in return for yours.'

The morning of the third day's sport was a merry one. The earth was all whitened with frost, and the sun rose on red drifting clouds. The sound of the horns in the woods made the rocks ring. A hound started up a fox and the hunt followed him fast. Reynard the fox dodged and doubled. And all this time Gawayn at the castle was sleeping uneasily.

That morning the lady came to him in a fair mantle trimmed with fur. Gawayn was troubled with sad thoughts, drooping in a dream about what should befall the next day.

'Sir Gawayn!' said the lady.

Gawayn stirred and woke.

'Forgive me, lady. I was dreaming.'

'Sir Gawayn, for the last time I beg you not to go to seek for the green chapel.'

'Lady, I must go. Not for you, nor for any lady alive, could I fail in this quest.'

'Well, if you must go I shall give you a gift before we part.'

Quickly the lady unfastened a girdle of green silk and gold which was tied about her waist.

'Take this,' she said.

'No. I thank you, lady, but I want no gift from you.'

'You refuse this belt? It seems a small thing, but it contains magic powers. No knight under heaven can cut down the man who wears this green belt. He cannot be slain.'

'He cannot be slain? Then I will wear the belt, fair lady, and fear the green knight no more.'

'Let me tie the girdle upon you, Sir Gawayn. And with it I shall give you three kisses. But do not show the girdle to my lord, I beg you. Wear it secretly when you meet the green knight.'

'I will do as you say, lady.'

Then Gawayn rose and dressed and made him merry with the ladies of the castle with comely carols and all kinds of joy. And at last dark night fell, the hunters came home, and the lord strode into the hall.

'Well,' he cried, 'back we come to the fire and the feast!'

'And I shall fulfil my part of the bargain first,' said Gawayn.

He embraced the lord and kissed him three times.

'You did better than I, sir knight,' said the lord. 'I have hunted all day and got nothing but this foul fox skin – the fiend take it! And that's a poor exchange for the kisses you have given me. Now let us be as merry as we can, for tomorrow you go to the green chapel.'

'Yes,' answered Gawayn. 'Tomorrow I go to the green chapel.'

The night-time passed and the New Year came. The world wakened to wild weather. Clouds cast keen cold to the earth. The bitter snow came shivering down. And the wind rushed over the sky, blowing shrilly and filling every valley with great snowdrifts.

Gawayn slept little. At last the cock crowed. It was the appointed day. He got up before daylight and dressed by the light of a lamp. He ordered that Gringolet should be saddled, and he put on his armour. But first he tied the lady's girdle about his waist.

Then he bade farewell to the lord and his lady.

'I commend this castle to Christ,' he said.

The drawbridge was let down, the broad gates unbarred, and Gawayn rode forth alone except for the servant who was to show him the way to the green chapel.

They went by banks where the boughs were bare. They climbed by cliffs where the cold clung. Mist drizzled on the moor and melted on the mountains. Each hill had a hat and a huge mist-cloak. They took a wandering way by a wood, until at daybreak they were standing on a high hill, with white snow about them.

'Now, my lord,' said the servant, 'you are not far from the perilous place you wanted to find. There in the green chapel lives the worst man on earth. He is stiff and stern and he loves to strike, and if any knight passes by the chapel he dings him to death. Therefore, good Sir Gawayn, let that man alone. Take some other path where Christ may speed you. And I shall hie me home again and never tell that you fled from the green knight.'

'No,' said Gawayn. 'If I were to fly I would be a coward knight. I must go to the chapel.'

'Then here are your helmet and your spear, my lord. Ride down that path by the side of the rocks till you reach the bottom of the wild valley yonder. Then look a little on the field on the left hand. And in that valley you shall see the chapel and the strong man who guards it.'

'I thank you.'

'Fare you well. I would not go with you for all the gold upon earth. Farewell, Gawayn the noble.'

The servant set spurs to his horse and galloped away, leaving Gawayn alone.

'I will trust God,' said Gawayn to himself. Then he spurred Gringolet along the path and rode down to the valley.

When he got there he looked about him. It seemed a desolate place. There were high, steep banks on either side, and rough, rugged crags with gnarled stones. There was no sign of a green chapel. Except – what was that grassy mound at the edge of a stream beside a waterfall?

Gawayn tethered Gringolet to a tree. He went to the mound and walked round it.

'Is this the green chapel?' he mused. 'It is hollow inside. It seems like a cave or a crevice in a rock. I can imagine the devil holding a service here at midnight. It is the strangest church that ever I saw!'

Then he heard, coming from the high hill beyond the brook, a strange noise.

It whirred and ground, like water in a mill.

It rushed and rang, frightening to hear.

Gawayn called out, 'Who lives in this place? Here is good Sir Gawayn come to this chapel. If any man wants me, let him come now or never!'

'Abide!' cried a voice from the bank above his head.

'Ay will I,' said Gawayn. 'Come out, green knight.'

'Abide!' said the voice again. 'And you shall have what I promised you once. Stand fast, Sir Gawayn!'

Then the huge green knight came whirling out of a hole in a rock with a terrible weapon, a sharp axe with which to give the blow.

'You are welcome to my place, Gawayn,' he said. 'You know the bargain we made. At this New Year I return the blow you gave me. Take your helm from your head and have here your pay.'

'Strike then,' said Gawayn.

He bowed his head and waited. The green knight gathered up his grim axe to smite Gawayn. But Gawayn looked sideways at the axe as it came gliding down and shrank his neck from the sharp iron. The knight held back the blade with a jerk and spoke scornfully.

'Surely you cannot be Gawayn, to flinch before you feel any harm. I did not flinch at the court of King Arthur. My head flew to my foot, but still I fled not. So I should be called the better man.'

'I shrank once,' said Gawayn. 'I shall not shrink again. Deal me my blow.'

'Have at thee, then!'

The green knight raised his axe and took a swing at Gawayn. But again he did not strike. He held back the axe before it did any harm, while Gawayn stood as still as a stone.

'So, now you have found your courage again,' said the green knight.

'Strike on!' answered Gawayn. 'You threaten too long.'

Then the green knight set himself to strike. But though he struck fiercely, he did not hurt Gawayn. He cut him slightly, and red blood fell to the earth. When Gawayn saw his blood on the snow he sprang away more than a spear's length. He whipped out his bright sword and fiercely he spoke.

'That is enough, knight. I have borne one stroke as our bargain said. If you deal any more I shall avenge it, and swiftly too.'

'Not so fierce, valiant knight,' said the green knight merrily in a loud, ringing voice. 'Now, Sir Gawayn, where is your girdle?'

'The girdle?'

'Yes, the belt which was woven by my own wife. I am the lord of the castle, Sir Gawayn. Thrice you paid me back my wife's kisses, giving all you gained, as a good man should.

So thrice I held my axe from your neck. But she gave you a girdle and you hid it. And for that I nicked your neck a little.'

Gawayn stood for a while in shame.

'Cursed be my greed and cowardice!' he said at last. 'Here, take the girdle, ill luck go with it! I am both faulty and false.'

The green knight laughed.

'No no. You are a true knight. When my wife tried to turn aside your purpose you did not listen. You faithfully came to the green chapel.'

'But I kept the girdle. And I hid it from you.'

'That is now amended. You had your punishment at the edge of my axe. And I give you the girdle hemmed with gold, for it is as green as my gown.'

'I thank you, lord. I shall gladly keep the girdle. Not for the silk or the gold, but to remind me of my fault. When I am too proud of my prowess in arms I shall look at this girdle and become humble again. But one thing I would ask since you are the lord of the castle. What is your name?'

'I am called Sir Bercilak of the green chapel. Now come and make merry at my castle. Let us revel the New Year out.'

'I thank you, but I must go back to King Arthur's Court.'

'Farewell then, Gawayn. God be your guide.'

'Farewell, Sir Bercilak.'

Wild ways of the world Gawayn now rode, wearing the shining belt around him to show his guilt. And so he came safely back to King Arthur's court, and told the tale of his adventures.

And when he had told everything the knights of the Round Table all agreed that each should wear a bright green girdle about him for the sake of Gawayn.

That is the way this adventure happened in the time of King Arthur.

Geoffrey Chaucer

The Franklin's Tale

THERE was once a knight called Arveragus who lived in Brittany with his wife Dorigen, the fairest lady under the sun. Arveragus and Dorigen loved one another dearly, and lived together in great joy.

But when they had been married for a year or more Arveragus made up his mind to go to England to seek honour in arms. There he meant to stay for a year or two.

Now Dorigen loved her husband as much as she loved her life. When he went away she wept, and sighed, and moaned. She could neither eat nor sleep. The whole wide world seemed as nothing to her without Arveragus.

Her friends did their best to comfort her. And gradually, indeed, her grief grew less. When they saw this, her friends begged her to go out and try to drive away any dark thoughts. At last she agreed.

The castle where Dorigen lived stood close to the sea. And as she walked on the cliffs she could see ships sailing by. This made her unhappy once more.

'Alas!' she said. 'Will none of these many ships bring home my lord to me?'

Then again she would sit on the green turf and look down over the edge of the cliff. Below her she saw grisly black rocks which made her heart quake for fear. And looking at the sea she would say with sorrowful sighs:

'O God, men say you have made nothing in vain. But these fiendish rocks do no good to man, nor bird, nor beast. Thousands of men have been driven by the wind against the rocks, and drowned. So for my lord's sake I wish these black rocks were sunk into hell. They slay me with fear.'

Thus Dorigen spoke, weeping bitterly.

Her friends saw that it did her harm to walk by the sea. So one morning they took her to a lovely garden where they were going to enjoy themselves the whole day long.

It was early in May. And the month of May with its gentle showers had painted the garden all over with flowers and leaves.

After dinner the guests began to dance and sing. All except Dorigen. She had no wish to dance, for the husband whom she loved so dearly was not there.

Now among the dancers there was a squire called Aurelius. He was young, strong, rich, wise and well-loved by his friends. And for two years and more Aurelius had been in love with Dorigen, although Dorigen did not know it.

But before they left the garden, Aurelius, whose home was near Dorigen's castle, went up to Dorigen and began to talk to her. And as they spoke together Aurelius could not help saying something of what was in his heart.

'Madam,' he said at last, 'one word from you can kill me or save me. Have pity on me, sweet one. I am dying for love of you.'

Dorigen looked at him.

'I never knew it before,' she said. 'But I will tell you this, Aurelius. I could not be untrue to Arveragus. This is my final answer.'

Then she added a few words in jest.

'Aurelius,' she said, 'I will take you for my love if you remove all the rocks which stand along the coast of Brittany, so that they can no longer harm the ships that sail on the sea.'

'Have you no more mercy than this?' said he.

'No, by the Lord who made me,' said she. 'And I know well that such a thing will never happen. Forget this folly. I am the wife of another man.'

Aurelius went back to his house with a sorrowful heart. And for two years and more he lay in his bed, suffering torments of misery. Only his brother, who was a clerk, knew about his woe and the cause of it.

Meanwhile Arveragus came triumphantly home. There was dancing and jousting, and he and Dorigen lived together with much happiness.

All this time Aurelius' brother grieved in secret, and wondered how to help Aurelius. At last he remembered that when he had been in Orleans as a young scholar he had come upon a book of magic. And when he thought of this book his heart began to dance for joy.

'My brother shall soon be cured!' he cried. 'He shall be cured by magic arts. I have heard it said that at feasts magicians can fill a great hall with water. And a barge comes gliding in upon the water and is rowed up and down. Then the water disappears and a grim lion comes. Or flowers blossom as though in a meadow. Or a vine grows, with white and purple grapes. Or a stone castle towers up, and then disappears again at the magician's will. If I went to Orleans, I might find someone who could banish the black rocks of Brittany for a day or two. Then Dorigen would have to keep her promise.'

The brother went to where Aurelius lay in bed. And he gave him such hope that he rose up, and the two of them travelled to Orleans.

When they had almost reached the city they met a young scholar roaming by himself.

'I know the cause of your coming,' he said. And he told them all that was in their minds.

So Aurelius and his brother went to the house of this magician. And before they had supper he showed them many things. He showed them forests full of wild deer with great antlers which were being hunted by hounds and slain with arrows. Then the deer disappeared, and they saw falconers on the banks of a fair river who had killed a heron with their hawks. Next they saw knights jousting on a plain. And after that the magician showed Aurelius his lady Dorigen dancing, and it seemed to Aurelius that he himself was dancing with her.

Then the magician clapped his hands. And farewell! the sport was over.

Now all this time they had never moved from the magician's house. They had sat quietly in his study where his books were, with no man present but the three of them.

When they had supped they discussed what the magician's reward should be if he removed all the rocks of Brittany. And the magician said that Aurelius would have to give him a thousand pounds.

'Fie on a thousand pounds!' cried Aurelius. 'I would give the whole wide world to have Dorigen for my love. You shall be paid. But keep us here no longer than tomorrow.'

'No, on my faith,' said the magician.

The next day as soon as it was light they set out for Brittany.

Now Aurelius begged the magician to do his best to ease his pain. And the magician felt such pity for Aurelius that he worked night and day. He sat over his magic books and his calculations, and at last, through his magic, for a week or two it seemed that all the rocks on the coast of Brittany had disappeared.

When Aurelius heard this he knelt down at the magician's feet. 'Thank you, lord,' he said. 'You have helped me out of my cold cares.'

Then he hastened to a place where he knew he would see Dorigen. And when she came along he greeted her timidly and humbly.

'Madam,' he said, 'do you remember what you promised me once in the garden yonder? You promised that you would love me if I removed all the rocks which stand along the coast of Brittany. Well, I have done as you commanded. Go and see for yourself. The rocks have all vanished.'

With that Aurelius went away, and Dorigen stood there, pale and aghast. Never had she imagined that she would be trapped like this.

'Alas that this should happen!' she said. 'I did not think that such a monstrous thing could come to be. It is quite against nature.'

Dorigen went home and wept and wailed. Arveragus was away, but in her sorrow she spoke aloud.

'I must choose between death and dishonour,' she said. 'I cannot be untrue to Arveragus. It would be better to kill myself.'

On the third night Arveragus came home and asked Dorigen why she wept so sorely. 'Alas that ever I was born!' said she. And she told Arveragus the whole story.

Arveragus spoke gently to her.

'Is that all, Dorigen?' he said. 'You do not love this man?'

'No! No! And I never will.'

'Well, what is done is done, wife. And on my word you must keep your promise. I love you too much to prevent you from doing that.'

Then he began to weep bitterly.

'I will bear my sorrow as best I can,' he said. 'Tell no one what has happened. I will keep a cheerful face lest anyone should think harm of you.'

And he called a squire and a maiden.

'Go forth with Dorigen,' he said. 'Take her to the place where she must go.'

So Dorigen made her way towards the garden where she had given her promise to Aurelius. Aurelius had watched her leave her castle, as he often did, and he met her in the busiest street of the town.

'Where are you going, lady?' he asked.

Dorigen answered, distracted with grief.

'I am going to the garden, as my husband bade me. I am going to keep my promise, alas! alas!'

Aurelius began to think what he should do. He was filled with pity for Dorigen and for Arveragus who had nobly told her to keep her promise. And it seemed to him that it would be better to give up Dorigen than to behave unworthily.

'Madam,' he said, 'tell your lord Arveragus that I would rather be sorrowful for ever than part you from your husband. And I take my leave of the truest and best wife I have ever known. A squire can do a noble deed as well as a knight.'

Dorigen fell upon her knees and thanked Aurelius. Then she went home to her husband and told him what had happened. And he and she lived happily together again.

Aurelius, left alone, cursed the day on which he was born.

'How shall I pay the magician a thousand pounds in

gold?' he said. 'I shall have to sell my goods and become a beggar. But whatever happens I shall keep my part of the bargain.'

With a sore heart he went to the chest where he kept his money and took out five hundred pounds worth of gold. Then he brought it to the magician.

'Master,' he said, 'I have never yet broken my word. I shall pay my debt even if I must go a-begging. But if you would give me two or three years to pay the rest, then I need not sell my property.'

'Have I kept our agreement?' asked the magician gravely.

'Well and truly.'

'Have you won your lady?'

'No,' answered Aurelius with a sigh.

'Why not? Tell me.'

Aurelius told him all that had happened.

'Arveragus would rather die in misery,' he said, 'than let his wife fail in her promise.'

He spoke, too, of Dorigen's sorrow.

'I had such great pity on her,' he said, 'that I sent her back to Arveragus again as generously as he had sent her to me.'

'Each of you behaved nobly to the other,' said the magician. 'You are a squire, and Arveragus is a knight. I am a scholar, and God forbid that a scholar should not do a noble deed as well as either of you.'

'What do you mean?'

'Sir, I release you from paying me a thousand pounds. I will not take a penny from you, in spite of all my trouble. Farewell! Good day to you!'

And the magician took his horse and rode off.

Now which of these people was the most generous? What do you think?

Sir Thomas Malory

Gareth and Lynette

At the time of the feast of Pentecost King Arthur was in one of his castles with the knights of the Round Table. Now when there was a feast Arthur never liked to sit at meat until he had heard or seen some great marvel.

A little before noon on the day of Pentecost Sir Gawayn was looking out of a window when he saw three horsemen approaching and a dwarf on foot. The horsemen alighted outside the castle, while the dwarf held the horses.

Then Sir Gawayn went to the king.

'Sir,' he said, 'you can go to your meat. For here close at hand come strange adventures.'

So Arthur sat down in the great hall of the castle with the knights of the Round Table.

Presently two men came into the hall with a third man supported between them. The man who leaned on their shoulders was young and handsome, tall and strong. And yet it seemed that he could not walk by himself.

Without any word these men went up to the high table where Arthur sat. Then the young man stretched up straight and stood alone.

'God bless you and all your knights, King Arthur,' he said. 'I have come here to ask you to give me three gifts. One gift I shall ask for now, and the other two a year hence.'

'Ask,' said Arthur, 'and you shall have what you wish.'

'I ask that for a year you will give me sufficient meat and drink.'

'Ask better,' said Arthur. 'This is but simple asking, and surely you are of noble birth.'

'I have asked what I will ask,' replied the young man.

'Well,' said the king, 'you shall have meat and drink enough. But tell me – what is your name?'

'Ah, that I cannot tell.'

Then the king told Sir Kay the steward to give the young man the best meat and drink, and to treat him as though he were a lord's son.

'He is no lord's son,' said Sir Kay. 'If he were, he would have asked for a horse and armour. And since he has no name I will give him one. I shall call him Fair Hands.'

Then the two men went away and left the young man with Sir Kay, who scorned and mocked him.

Time passed, and the young man was ever meek and mild, and did what Sir Kay told him. He worked in the kitchen with the other kitchen boys. But whenever there was any jousting of knights he saw it if he could.

And through this time Sir Gawayn and Sir Launcelot were always kind to the youth whom Sir Kay called Fair Hands. When Sir Kay mocked him, Sir Launcelot bade him leave his mocking.

'For,' he said, 'I would wager my head he shall prove a man of great honour.'

And always Sir Launcelot gave him gold to spend, and clothes, and so did Sir Gawayn. Sir Gawayn did this because of the tie of blood, for he was nearer kin to Fair Hands than he knew. But Sir Launcelot did it from his great gentleness and courtesy.

Then came the feast of Pentecost again. And the king would eat no meat until he had seen some marvel.

Soon a squire came to King Arthur and said:

'Sir, you may go and eat. For here comes a damsel with some strange adventures.'

The king was glad, and he sat down in his hall with his knights.

Then a lady entered the hall and went up to the king.

'I need help, King Arthur,' she said.

'For whom?' asked the king. 'What is the adventure?'

'It is this,' said the lady. 'I am the lady Lynette. My sister, the lady Liones, is besieged in her castle by a knight called the Red Knight of the Red Lawns.'

'I know him not,' said the king.

'Sir, I know him well,' said Sir Gawayn. 'He is one of the most perilous knights of the world.'

'Fair lady,' said Arthur, 'there are many knights here who would rescue the lady of whom you speak.'

At that Fair Hands came before the king.

'I have been a twelvemonth in your kitchen, sir king,' he said. 'And now I ask for my other two gifts. Grant me this adventure, and let Sir Launcelot ride after me and make me a knight when I require it.'

'You shall have your gifts,' said the king.

But Lynette was much displeased.

'Fie on you!' she cried. 'Are you sending a kitchen boy to help me?'

And she rode away in anger.

Then the dwarf who had come with Fair Hands before came to the court with a horse so fine and armour so rich that everyone marvelled. And Fair Hands put on the armour and rode after the lady.

'He is only a kitchen boy,' sneered Sir Kay. 'I will ride after him and see whether he will know me for his better.'

So Sir Kay took his horse and spear and rode after Fair Hands, and Sir Launcelot followed. And just as Fair Hands overtook the lady, Sir Kay came up to him.

'What sir, do you not know me?' cried Sir Kay.

Fair Hands turned his horse and saw that it was Sir Kay who had mocked him all that year.

'Yea,' he said. 'I know you for an ungentle knight of the court. Beware of me!'

Fair Hands had neither spear nor shield, and Sir Kay rode straight at him with his spear. But Fair Hands came at Sir Kay with his sword in his hand and put away the spear with his sword, and wounded Sir Kay, and unhorsed him.

Then Fair Hands dismounted and took Sir Kay's shield and spear and got upon his own horse again. Sir Launcelot saw all this, and so did Lynette.

'Will you fight with me, Sir Launcelot?' cried Fair Hands.
'If you wish.'

So Fair Hands and Launcelot fought, first on horses and then on foot. They rushed together like boars, tracing and racing, and Launcelot felt that Fair Hands was fighting more like a giant than a knight.

'Fight not so sore, Fair Hands,' he gasped. 'Your quarrel and mine is not so great that we may not leave off.'

'Am I fit to be made a knight?' asked Fair Hands.

'Yea, truly.'

'Then give me the order of knighthood.'

'I must know your name first,' said Launcelot.

'You will tell no one?' asked Fair Hands.

'I promise I shall not tell until it is openly known,' answered Sir Launcelot.

'My name is Gareth,' said Fair Hands. 'I am the son of King Lot of Orkney and Queen Morgawse his wife. And I am brother to Sir Gawayn, although he did not know me.'

'I always thought you were of noble blood,' said Sir Launcelot. And he gave Gareth the order of knighthood.

Sir Kay was carried on his shield back to the court, where everyone mocked him. But Sir Gareth rode on.

When he had overtaken Lynette she spoke to him in anger.

'What are you doing here, cookboy?' she cried. 'Your clothes are stained with grease and tallow. You stink of the kitchen.'

'Lady,' said Gareth, 'say to me what you will. I shall not leave you. For I have promised King Arthur to take on your adventure, and I shall finish it to the end or die.'

'Then you will meet a knight so bold that you will never dare to look him in the face.'

'I shall try,' said Gareth.

So they rode on, and encountered many adventures. Gareth slew six thieves and freed a knight who had been captured by them. He killed two knights who tried to stop him from crossing a great river. He slew a knight called the Black Knight of the Black Lawns, and encountered his brother the Green Knight who promised to serve him in any way he could. He overcame a third brother, the Blue Knight, and this brother too promised to do him service.

And through all these adventures Lynette mocked and taunted him.

'Cookboy! Ladlewasher!' she would cry. 'Wretched knave, you are nothing but a scullion.'

'Say what you will, lady,' Gareth replied. 'Wherever you go I will follow you.'

But at last, when she saw how bravely he bore himself, the lady repented and spoke more kindly to Sir Gareth.

'I marvel,' she said, 'what manner of man you be. For never did a woman treat a knight so foully and shamefully as I have you. And ever courteously you have suffered it.'

'Lady,' said Gareth, 'I took little heed to your words. Indeed the more you said the more you angered me, and I wreaked my wrath upon the knights with whom I fought. So all you said against me helped me in my battles.'

'Forgive me, Fair Hands,' said the lady.

'With all my heart,' said Sir Gareth. 'And if you will not give away my secret I will tell you who I am. My name is Gareth of Orkney, and King Lot was my father, and my mother is King Arthur's sister, Dame Morgawse. And Sir Gawayn is my brother, though I am younger far than he.'

'Then I was right,' said Lynette. 'You are indeed of noble blood.'

Now Gareth and Lynette rode through a forest and came to a plain where there were many pavilions and tents and a fair castle. The sea beat upon one side of the castle walls, and there were many ships and much noise of mariners calling to one another with 'Hey!' and 'Ho!'

'Now we have come to the Castle Perilous,' said Lynette to Sir Gareth. 'This is where the Red Knight of the Red Lawns is besieging my sister Dame Liones.'

Near the castle there was a sycamore tree, and on it hung a great horn made of ivory.

Sir Gareth spurred his horse straight to the sycamore tree, and blew the horn so eagerly that the whole plain rang with the sound.

Knights came forth from the tents and pavilions, people looked out from the castle walls and windows, and the Red Knight of the Red Lawns armed himself hastily, ready to do battle.

'Sir,' said the lady Lynette to Sir Gareth, 'look up at that window of the castle. There is my sister, Dame Liones.'

Gareth looked up at the window and could not stop looking. 'She seems the fairest lady that ever I saw,' he said. 'I ask nothing better than to do battle for her.'

Then Gareth told the lady Lynette to go farther away, and he and the Red Knight put their spears ready and came together with all their might. They struck one another's shields with such force that they both fell to the earth, with the reins of their bridles in their hands. And the people in the castle and the knights who were besieging it thought that their necks were broken.

But at last they rose. And leaving their horses they held their shields before them, drew their swords, and ran together like two fierce lions. And they gave each other such buffets on their helms that they reeled two strides backwards. Then they recovered and went on hacking and hewing.

Thus they fought until it was past noon and they had no breath left. They stood wagging and staggering, panting, blowing and bleeding so that all who saw them wept for pity. Then they rested and went to battle again, tracing, racing and parrying like two boars.

Sometimes they ran back and hurtled together like rams fighting, and they fell grovelling to the earth. Sometimes they were so confused that each took the other's sword instead of his own.

At last the Red Knight smote Sir Gareth so that his sword fell out of his hand. Then he gave Gareth a buffet on the helm which felled him to the ground. And next he lay on him to hold him down.

'O Sir Gareth, where is your courage gone?' cried Lynette. 'My sister is watching you and she sobs and weeps to see you.'

When Sir Gareth heard this he gathered his strength and got to his feet. He took his sword in his hand and doubled his strokes upon the Red Knight so that at last he struck him down. And the Red Knight cried out with a loud voice:

'O noble knight, I yield to your mercy.'

Then Sir Gareth bade the Red Knight go to the lady Liones and ask her to forgive him for all he had done against her.

And when the lady Lynette had cared for his wounds Sir Gareth armed himself and took his spear and rode to the Castle Perilous to see Dame Liones.

But when he came to the gate he found many armed men there, and the drawbridge was pulled up. He looked up to the window, and there he saw the lady Liones.

'Go away, Fair Hands,' she said. 'I cannot love you until I know that you are worthy of my love.'

And she turned from the window, while Gareth rode away in great sorrow.

But the lady thought much about Fair Hands, and she called to her Sir Gringamour her brother.

'Ride after Fair Hands,' she said. 'And if you find him sleeping take his dwarf and bring him to me. For my sister Lynette says that the dwarf can tell me Fair Hands' right name.'

So Sir Gringamour rode until he found Sir Gareth lying asleep by a lake, with his head upon his shield. And he came stilly stalking behind the dwarf, and plucked him fast under his arm, and rode away.

But as he rode, the dwarf cried to his master for help. And Gareth woke and armed himself and followed Sir Gringamour.

He rode through marshes and fields and great dales, for he did not know the way. And at last he met a poor countryman.

'Good morrow,' he said. 'Have you seen a knight upon a black horse, and a little dwarf sitting behind him with heavy cheer?'

'Sir,' said the countryman, 'Sir Gringamour the knight passed by me with a dwarf mourning as you say. And the castle he rides to is but two miles hence.'

So Gareth rode on.

Meanwhile the dwarf had told Dame Liones that Gareth was a king's son. And when Gareth reached the Castle Perilous, Dame Liones came forth arrayed like a princess, and promised to love Gareth and none other all the days of her life.

Now the Green Knight had come to King Arthur's court with fifty knights and yielded to King Arthur. And the Blue Knight came with a hundred knights and the Red Knight of the Red Lawns with six hundred knights. And they all said that they had been sent by a knight called Fair Hands.

'He was with me for a year,' said King Arthur. 'And I marvel what blood he comes of, to fight so valiantly.'

Then as Arthur sat at meat, the Queen of Orkney, Queen Morgawse, came into the hall with a great number of ladies and knights.

'What have you done with my young son Gareth, brother?' she cried. 'He was here among you for a year, and you made a kitchen knave of him. Shame on you all!'

'O dear mother,' said Sir Gawayn, 'I did not know him.'

'Nor I,' said the king. 'And I shall never be glad till I find him.'

Sir Launcelot advised the king to send a messenger to Dame Liones, so that she might counsel him where to find Sir Gareth. And at Sir Gareth's wish the lady Liones held a tournament at her castle and said that whichever knight proved himself best there should have her hand.

So the tournament was held and King Arthur came with all his knights. And there Sir Gareth did marvellous deeds of arms. But no one knew him, for Dame Liones had lent him a ring which caused him to turn all manner of colours, now green, now red, now blue.

But at last when Sir Gareth went aside from the tournament for a moment his dwarf said to him:

'Leave me your ring, lest you should lose it while you drink and rest.'

When Sir Gareth had refreshed himself he rode eagerly to the field again, forgetting the ring. And one of King Arthur's heralds rode as near Sir Gareth as he could, so that he saw written about Gareth's helm in gold 'This is the helm of Sir Gareth of Orkney.'

Then all the heralds cried: 'This is Sir Gareth of Orkney, King Lot's son!'

And King Arthur rejoiced to see his nephew, and Sir Gawayn to see his brother. And as Sir Gareth had proved the best knight at the tournament he won the hand of the lady Liones.

So they were wedded on Michaelmas Day with great joy. And thus ends this tale of Sir Gareth of Orkney who wedded Dame Liones of the Castle Perilous.

Sir Thomas Malory

The Death of Arthur

KING Arthur fought against Sir Mordred who was his own son, on a down beside Salisbury not far from the seaside. Sir Mordred had a grim host of a hundred thousand men. And never was there a dolefuller battle in any Christian land.

They fought all the long day and never stopped till the noble knights of the Round Table lay on the cold earth. And ever they fought still till it was near night. And by that time there were a hundred thousand laid dead upon the down.

Then at last King Arthur gave Sir Mordred his death wound, and Sir Mordred smote his father Arthur with his sword in both hands. And the noble Arthur fell in a swoon to the earth.

Sir Lucan and Sir Bedivere his brother led him between them both to a little chapel. Sir Lucan was grievously wounded in many places, and in helping the king he fell dead.

'Alas,' said the king, 'this duke died for my sake, and he had more need of help than I. He would not complain, for his heart was so set to help me. Jesus have mercy upon his soul!'

Then Sir Bedivere wept for the death of his brother.

'Leave this mourning and weeping,' said the king, 'if I might live myself, the death of Sir Lucan would grieve me evermore. But my time hieth fast.'

So Arthur spoke again to Sir Bedivere.

'Take Excalibur my good sword,' he said, 'and go with it to the side of yonder water. And when you get there I bid you throw my sword in that water, and come again and tell me what you see there.'

'My lord,' said Sir Bedivere, 'I will do your commandment and swiftly bring you word again.'

So Bedivere departed. And as he went he looked at that noble sword and saw that the pommel and the hilt were all of precious stones.

Then he said to himself:

'If I throw this rich sword in the water no good shall come of it. It will only be lost.'

And Sir Bedivere hid Excalibur under a tree. And so, as quickly as he could, he returned to the king.

'I have been to the water's edge,' he said. 'I have thrown in the sword.'

'What did you see there?' asked the king.

'Sir,' said Sir Bedivere, 'I saw nothing but waves and winds.'

'Then you are lying,' said the king. 'You did not throw in the sword. Therefore go speedily again and do my bidding. As you are dear to me, spare not, but throw it in.'

Then Sir Bedivere went back and took the sword in his hand. And still it seemed to him a sin and a shame to throw in that noble sword. And he hid it, and returned to the king and told him that he had been at the water and had done his bidding.

'What did you see there?' said the king.

'Sir,' he said, 'I saw nothing but the waters wap and the waves wan.'

'Ah, lying traitor,' said King Arthur. 'Now you have betrayed me twice. Who would have believed it, you who have been so dear to me? You are known as a noble knight,

Sir Bedivere, and you would betray me for the richness of a sword. Go again quickly. Your long tarrying puts me in great danger of my life. For I have taken cold. And if you do not do as I bid you, I will slay you with my own hands. For you would see me dead for the sake of my rich sword.'

Then Sir Bedivere departed and went to where the sword was. And he swiftly took it up, and went to the water-side. And then he threw the sword as far into the water as he could.

And there came an arm and a hand above the water and met the sword, and caught it. And the hand shook the sword

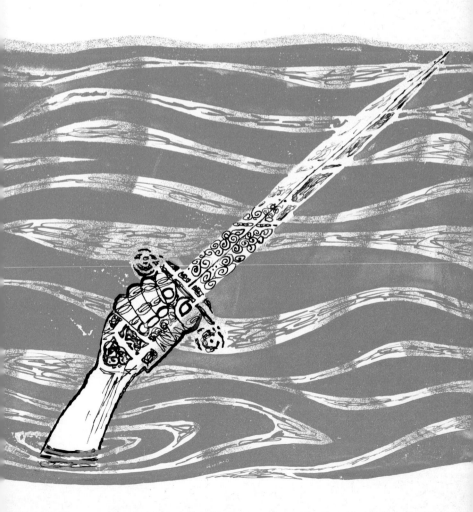

thrice and brandished it, and then vanished away with the sword into the water.

So Sir Bedivere came again to the king and told him what he saw.

'Alas,' said the king, 'help me away from here. For I fear I have tarried too long.'

Then Sir Bedivere took the king upon his back, and so went with him to that water-side. And when they were at the water-side, close by the bank there hove a little barge with many fair ladies in it. They all had black hoods. And they wept and shrieked when they saw King Arthur.

'Now put me into the barge,' said the king.

And Sir Bedivere softly put Arthur in. And three queens received him there with great mourning. And so they set him down, and in the lap of one of them King Arthur laid his head.

And then that queen said to Arthur:

'Ah, dear brother, why have you tarried so long from me? Alas, this wound in your head has caught over-much cold.'

And then they rowed away from the land, and Sir Bedivere saw all those ladies depart from him.

Then Sir Bedivere cried out:

'Ah my lord Arthur, what shall become of me, now you go from me and leave me here alone among my enemies?'

'Comfort yourself,' said the king. 'And do as well as you can, for you cannot put your trust in me. For I will go into the valley of Avilion to heal me of my grievous wound. And if you never hear more of me, pray for my soul.'

And all this time the queens and ladies wept and shrieked, so that it was pity to hear them.

And as soon as Sir Bedivere had lost sight of the barge he wept and wailed. Then he took to the forest, and travelled all night.

In the morning he came to a chapel and a hermitage set

between two ancient woods. Then he was glad, and went thither. And when he came to the chapel he saw a hermit lying there lamenting beside a newly-dug grave.

'Sir,' said Bedivere, 'what man is buried there that you pray for so earnestly?'

'Fair son,' said the hermit, 'I do not know for certain, but only by guessing. This night, at midnight, there came a number of ladies, and brought hither a dead corpse, and prayed me to bury him. And they offered here a hundred candles, and gave me a hundred gold coins.'

'Alas,' said Sir Bedivere, 'that was my lord Arthur, that lies here buried in this chapel.'

Then Sir Bedivere swooned, and when he awoke he prayed the hermit that he might stay with him there and live with fasting and prayers.

'For I will never willingly go hence,' said Sir Bedivere. 'But all the days of my life I will pray here for my lord Arthur.'

'You are welcome to me,' said the hermit, 'for I know you better than you think I do. You are the bold Bedivere, and the noble duke Sir Lucan was your brother.'

Then Sir Bedivere told the hermit all that you have already heard.

So there Sir Bedivere lived with the hermit. And he put on poor clothes, and served the hermit humbly with fasting and prayers.

More of the death of King Arthur I could never find, but that ladies brought him to his burial.

Yet some men say in many parts of England that King Arthur is not dead, but taken by the will of our Lord Jesus to another place. And men say that he shall come again.

I will not say it shall be so, but rather I will say, here in this world he changed his life.

For those who would like
to know more about the stories

THE FOX AND THE WOLF
THE COUNTRY MOUSE AND THE TOWN MOUSE
THE LION AND THE MOUSE

These tales come from the *Morall Fabilles of Esope* by
Robert Henryson (?1430–1506). We know little about
Henryson's life except that he was a schoolmaster at Dun-
fermline. Henryson's *Fabilles* are adaptations of popular
tales about animals, and many of them are not Aesop's. They
are told in verse in a homely, humorous, easy way which
gives them great charm.

> 'The hartlie joy God geve ye had sene
> Beis kith quhen that thir sisteris met!
> And grit kyndnes wes schawin thame betuene,
> For quylis thay leuch, and quylis for joy thay gret,
> Quyle kissit sweit, quylis in armis plet.'

> 'If only you could have seen the joy when those two sisters met!
> They laughed, they cried, they kissed, they hugged each other.'

SIR ORFEO

Sir Orfeo appears to have been translated from a French
story into south-western English – though some scholars
disagree about the dialect – at the beginning of the fourteenth
century. With a light and deft touch it tells the story of
Orpheus and Eurydice. This tale was known to the Middle
Ages chiefly from Ovid and Virgil. But in *Sir Orfeo* the
original Greek myth dissolves into a delicate fairy tale which

is given a happy ending. All through the story the classical background is adapted to a mediaeval setting. Here are knights and ladies, banquets in hall on trestle tables, hawking and hunting.

> 'He might se him bisides
> Oft in hot undertides
> The king o fairy with his rout
> Com to hunt him al about.
> With dim cri and bloweing.'

> 'On hot days he often saw the king of fairy with his followers hunting all about him. With faint cries and with horns blowing they rode.'

HAVELOK THE DANE

The lay – a narrative poem – of Havelok the Dane was discovered by accident in a manuscript belonging to the Bodleian Library in Oxford. The author is unknown. The manuscript is early fourteenth century; but the poem almost certainly belongs to the previous century. There is reason to believe that it was written in Lincolnshire, which is the scene of part of the tale. Havelok is full of Norse words, and this is an additional reason for thinking that it was composed in a place such as Lincolnshire where Norse influence was strong.

Havelok must not be taken as belonging to history. It was a popular romance, and people enjoyed it for its story. Many mediaeval romances contain visions of conquests such as those described by Havelok.

> 'And mine armes weren so longe,
> That i fadmede, al at ones,
> Denemark, with mine longe bones.'

> 'And my arms were so long that I could encircle the whole of Denmark with them.'

GARETH AND LYNETTE
THE DEATH OF ARTHUR

These tales come from the *Morte D'Arthur* by Sir Thomas Malory. When Malory was imprisoned by King Edward the Fourth he decided to spend his time translating French romances. The result was the *Morte D'Arthur*, which Malory finished in 1469. It was printed by Caxton in 1485, fourteen years after Malory's death.

No scholar has been able to trace the source of the story of Gareth and Lynette, and it is thought that it may come from a French poem now lost. Not all Malory's sources were French, however. He seems to have known English books about Arthur as well, and traditions concerning Arthur which survived in the countryside.

> 'Yet som men say in many partys of Inglonde that kynge Arthur ys nat dede, but had by the wyll of Oure Lorde Jesu into another place; and men say that he shall com agayne, and he shall wynne the Holy Crosse.'

THE DREAM OF MACSEN WLEDIG
THE FIRST GREAT DEED OF PEREDUR

These tales are taken from a collection of stories from Wales called the *Mabinogion*. They are written down in two Welsh collections – the White Book of Rhydderch (1300–25) and the Red Book of Hergest (1375–1425). But some of the stories must have been known a long time before the earliest of these manuscripts. *The Dream of Macsen Wledig* is delicately and skilfully written, and in it places and travels are carefully described. *Peredur* belongs to a later group of stories. It shows a Norman-French influence, in the characterization and background, in the clothes and armour described, and in the less detailed indications of the scenes where the action takes place. Here is a quotation from a later part of the long story of Peredur.

'A deu was ieueinc yn saethu karneu eu kyllyll o ascwrn morvil.'
'And two young lads throwing knives, and the hafts of their knives of walrus-ivory.'

SIR GAWAYN AND THE GREEN KNIGHT

This poem in the dialect of Cheshire or Lancashire is written on vellum in a small sharp hand. No one knows who wrote it, but it is undoubtedly the best of the alliterative romances – that is, those in which alliteration takes the place of rhyme. The poet clearly knows a good deal about life in a nobleman's household, about hunting, and about the armour and equipment of knights. He has a great gift for detailed description, and there are many human and humorous touches in his work. The date is probably towards the end of the fourteenth century. Observe the alliteration in the second line of the example given below.

'Where is now your sourquydrye and your conquestes,
Your gryndellayk and your greme, and your grete wordes?'

'Where are your pride and your conquests now,
Your fierceness, your wrath, your great words?'

THE CHILDREN OF LIR

The strange and beautiful story of the children of Lir is one of three famous tales from Ireland called *The Three Sorrows of Storytelling*. Though not found in any very early manuscript, its subject matter goes back to primitive times. Lir belonged to the People of Dana, mythical invaders of Ireland who had the nature of gods. This story is among those which describe the Danaans coming out of their fairy world, and being embraced by the influences of Christianity.

In the Welsh *Mabinogion* we find a mythical person called Llŷr who is connected with the Irish Lir. Llŷr-cester, now Leicester, was a centre of the worship of Llŷr.

'Fionuala' means 'the maid of the fair shoulder'.

THE FRANKLIN'S TALE

Geoffrey Chaucer (?1340–1400) began *The Canterbury Tales*, from which *The Franklin's Tale* is taken, about 1387. He never finished his masterpiece, though he probably worked on it throughout the last years of his life. A franklin was a free man, though not nobly born, and Chaucer represents the franklin of *The Canterbury Tales* as a well-to-do country gentleman. The franklin introduces his story as an old Breton lay, that is, a story written down from the songs of Breton minstrels. *The Franklin's Tale* with its imaginative descriptions, humour, and skilful narrative is a good example of Chaucer in his full maturity.

'He shewed hym, er he wente to sopeer,
Forestes, parkes ful of wilde deer;
Ther saugh he hertes with hir hornes hye,
The gretteste that evere were seyn with eye.
He saugh of hem an hondred slayn with houndes,
And somme with arwes blede of bittre woundes.'

'And before he went to supper he showed him forests, and parks full of wild deer. There he saw harts with their great antlers – the largest any man has ever seen. He saw a hundred of them being killed by hounds, and some bleeding from fierce arrow-wounds.'

THE BATTLE OF BANNOCKBURN

John Barbour was probably born at Aberdeen and in 1357 he was Archdeacon of that town. In 1375 he composed a poem called the *Bruce*, from which this extract is taken. In the *Bruce* Barbour describes the long struggle waged by

Scotland to gain her independence. Parts of the poem are tedious, but Barbour has the eye of an artist for detail, and is at his best describing scenes of vigorous action.

Though his work is written in the spirit of noble romance, Barbour prided himself on his historical accuracy. The language of his poem is the literary Scots of the Lowlands in his time.

'The Inglis men, in othir party,
That richt as angelis schane brichtly,
War nocht arayit on sic maner;
For all thair batalis sammyn wer
In a schiltrum.'

'Opposite them they could see the Englishmen in their companies, shining as brightly as angels. They were not spread out like the Scots, but were drawn up closely.'

ADRIAN AND BARDUS

John Gower (1330–1408) was a Londoner who came of a Kentish family. He knew Chaucer well. *Adrian and Bardus* comes from Gower's poem 'Confessio Amantis' which he completed in 1390. Although Gower's single stories can be delightful, he is often a dull writer. Chaucer aptly labelled him 'moral Gower'.

'And thus of thilke unkinde blod
Stant the memoire into this day,
Wherof that every wys man may
Ensamplen him, and take in mynde
What schame it is to ben unkinde;
Agein the which reson debateth,
And every creature it hateth.'

'And so the memory of that unkind character remains to this day, and every wise man can learn a lesson from this, and remember what a shame it is to be unkind, for reason argues against it and every creature hates it.'